Twenty-Twenty Vision

Paddy Bostock

A Wings ePress, Inc.
Historical Fiction Novel

Wings ePress, Inc.

Edited by: Jeanne Smith
Copy Edited by: Brian Hatfield
Executive Editor: Jeanne Smith
Cover Artist: Trisha FitzGerald-Jung
Images from Pexels (Kevin Bidwell von Pexels) and Pixabay.

All rights reserved

Wings ePress Books
www.wingsepress.com

Copyright © 2021 by: Paddy Bostock
ISBN-13: 978-1-61309-520-1
ISBN-10: 1-61309-520-1

Published In the United States Of America

Wings ePress Inc.
3000 N. Rock Road
Newton, KS 67114

Dedication

In memory of Dani, my wife, lover and best friend.

* * *

Prologue

What follows is an historical 'faction,' mixing facts (real things) with fiction (imaginary things) in an attempt to come to terms with the *annus horribilis* of 2020, whose defining hallmark was the Covid-19 pandemic that touched so many aspects of lives worldwide. Clearly, any attempt to address all of those would be an impossible task thousands of pages long, but underpinning them, two radically opposite extremes of human behaviour emerged as a response to the demands to which the bug exposed us.

The first of these was the selfless quotidian dedication of medical professionals and other carers in overflowing hospitals, who continued battling the virus in all its manifestations while themselves struggling to stay sane in face of the superhuman demands under which their vocation placed them. It is to them that hearts go out, although they are not an integral part of the storyline.

The same hearts do not go out to those in the second category, the political leaders and their advisers, whose self*ish*, cynical narcissism and hubristic ambition justified their ignoring or scorning scientific counsel and denying the existence of the virus in its early manifestations until it was too late. Instead, such signals were obfuscated and subordinated to political and economic expediency, thereby opening the sluice gates to a plague in which hundreds of thousands of citizens would die in needless misery. This story takes as prime examples of this phenomenon the dereliction of duty by the leaders of the USA and the UK and proposes for them appropriate fictional comeuppance—nemesis, call it what you will. Minor liberties have been taken with their names, but such is the nature of faction.

One

It was as a result of pique at not being given what he considered a richly deserved knighthood for dedicated service to his country as architect of the 2016 Brexit victory that Norman Gubbins, chief (and only) adviser to Prime Minister Bruno Junkett, took his first step towards revenge. The benefits of being a Svengali were all very well, but there came a time when a fellow deserved proper public recognition. To this end, he had devised what he conceived of as a wakey-wakey call for his master to remind him who had *really* been pulling the strings for the last four years, to appreciate his oversights, and seek to make amends. *If*, and it was a big if, Junkett were able to put two and two together, and for once in his sweet life get four, Norman would be prepared to bin the plan he had in mind. But had the PM ever listened when Norman repeatedly put the case for his ennoblement? Not a chance.

"Terribly sorry, old chap. Busy, busy, busy as you can see," he would say each of the approximately twenty-seven times Norman had raised the subject, shuffling and riffling important-looking papers which Norman knew only too well to be a subterfuge, because Junkett normally relied on other people to read important papers and give him ten-word-only résumés in case he absolutely *had* to make a decision about their contents.

So it was that after one brush-off too many, Norman decided to activate his wake-up plan and let the devil take the hindmost, '*hind*most' being the operative word, seeing as it was in the bottom Norman intended shooting Bruno. Not in any obvious way such as with a gun, of course, that would be far too unsubtle and far too likely to lead to Norman's incarceration. No, no, what he had availed himself of was 10 Downing Street's advanced lavatory system into which he had installed in the post-number-two bottom-washing facility a secret dart he had wheedled out of chums of his in the military, claiming scientific interest in such arcane weaponry. This he could activate from an app on his phone to shoot into the exact spot he wanted on the defecator's backside. Once installed in its target, the dart was programmed to suck out whatever musculature or flab surrounded it and render the area, if not totally defunct, at least inconvenient when it came to sitting, standing, riding horses, bicycles and so on. Having covertly completed these preparations, all Norman had to do was await a fitting opportunity and it would be goodbye bumptious ingratitude and hello Wobbly Bum.

It was with some glee, therefore, that after yet another failed attempt to address the knighthood question with the solipsist he had steered through the Brexit victory and then crisis after crisis to the top job in the land without the least recognition, that the latter suddenly farted for England, clutched his rear end, and announced he needed the lavatorium.

"For a poo," he explained, heading for the already primed Prime Minister Only facility.

"Okey *do*key," muttered Norman, prodding at the phone always ready in his left hand and bringing up the screen that would show the exact parameters of his target as, pants down, it lowered itself over the bowl.

"So here goes," he added when the flabby backside had finally made contact with the seat and writhed itself into position, causing Norman to grin and momentarily recall the bit in the only American novel he'd ever read—J.D. Salinger's *The Catcher in the Rye*—in which Holden Caulfield rates his classmate Ernest Morrow as being "about as sensitive as a goddam toilet seat."

Norman's target was the left buttock which, once the dart had done its work and vacuumed out any residual muscle or other fibres, would deflate like a punctured tyre and render that side of the PM's backside as flat as a pancake, thereby, in Norman's fantasy, rendering him as physically half-arsed as he was mentally. Poetic justice, Norman reckoned such a condition would be when, after ducking, diving and prevaricating for his entire career in politics, news might emerge of Junkett's singular form of disability and perhaps cause embarrassment, which for once could not merely be shrugged off or have lines drawn under it. What if, for example, during yet another grilling from the Leader of the Opposition in Prime Minister's Question Time, he were to sigh and sit down in protest as usual, only this time to slide ignominiously sideways along the front bench on his ruined buttock, thereby opening the condition to public scrutiny and ridicule?

Norman was still chuckling at the prospect when Junkett returned to his office tugging up his trousers and complaining, "*Some*thing or another's just bitten me on the bum. Must've been a bally wasp or giant mosquito or something,"

"Sorry to hear that, PM. Left cheek or right?" said Norman

"Not sure," said the PM, investigating his rear end with a hand.

Norman sighed. Was this or was this not a person who couldn't find his own arse with both hands, a person who couldn't be sure about *any*thing unless his soon-to-be-ex-chief (and only) adviser told him what he could be sure about?

"Well just point at which side hurts," he said.

"*This* one," whimpered the PM, jabbing at his already deflating left buttock. "And it seems to be shrinking."

Norman shrugged. "You'll probably need a prosthesis then."

"Pro's thesis? A whore's essay?" said Junkett, unable even at this awkward moment to distance himself from the hallmark witty wordplay of his Oxford Union debating days, which meant practically nobody including him ever knew what he was talking about.

Norman re-shrugged. "If push comes to shove."

"And me in my *prime*, and not only as in minister? Dolly birds not likely to fancy shagging a fellow with a false bottom, are they?"

"False *half* bottom, PM," Norman corrected but Junkett appeared not to notice. "Now how about we get back to business?" he added.

Bruno sighed, still tweaking his fast vanishing left buttock and cursing monster mosquitoes. "If we *must*."

Junkett didn't like business very much, preferring to offload responsibility for decisions onto the toadying ministers in his cabinet, letting them take the blame for any cock-ups, then, if push came to heave-ho, firing them to deflect criticism from him. Such is the way with the self-obsessed. "What is it *now*?"

"What you are going to do about the Covid bug. If you remember, you've already had a lockdown, then lifted it because you reckoned the beast had gone away, even though the WHO scientists were saying it was still knocking about all over the place, so what do you propose as your next advice to the country?" asked Norman in the futile hope of getting a straight answer.

"*Qu'ils mangent de la brioche*," said Bruno, who'd always rather fancied himself as the sort of chap Marie-Antoinette would have fancied as a bedmate.

"Let them eat cake?"

"God, my bottom's hurting," said Bruno, whose maximum concentration span on anybody but himself was around five minutes. As one newspaper columnist had commented in one of his "PM Buffoon" pieces, Bruno was *the* narcissist's narcissist with whom possibly only the madman in the White House could compete.

"Tough shit," said Norman, finally shucking off the accustomed Mister Nice Guy aspect of his PM-Whisperer role, standing and making to head for the door. "Get what's left of your arse in gear right now and sort out my knighthood, or I'm out of here."

Which alarmed Bruno. What would he *do* without Gubbins' brains, let alone his slogan-producing bot company whose output was bettered only by that of the madman in the Kremlin?

"Come back, Norman, come *back*. Don't leave me all alone," he yowled at the only person in Downing Street he couldn't sack because to do so would be the equivalent of a political lobotomy. Fine, so Bruno could ponce about the country uttering lies masquerading as amusing hyperbole, but without Norman, he would have no recourse to the joined-up strategic thinking and the populist positioning which had won him the Brexit vote, the leadership of the Tory party, and then the election that had catapulted him into 10 Downing Street. The very *last* thing Bruno needed at the height of the Covid-19 thingummy was for Norman to jump ship. What if even more citizens inconveniently started dying now the lockdown had been lifted and folk had been told to get out, take foreign holidays, have a good time, spend their money and take no notice of foreigners looking ill? In the last analysis, what mattered here was the health of the nation's economy, not that of its citizens. After all, it wouldn't matter *so* much if financially burdensome old people died but, as Junkett had belatedly reflected with Norman's assistance, what if younger ones did, too? And worse still…what if the filthy lefty press were to pin the blame on *him* should some new spike in the bug attack? In that circumstance, even the normally obsequious shiny-faced health minister might capitulate in face of the flak and jump ship before he was pushed, leaving Bruno to face the music. Which would be bad news, *very* bad news, the sort of hole he depended on Norman Gubbins to foresee and dig him out of.

"*Please*, Norman," he begged. "What's all this stuff about knighthoods, by the way? First I've heard of such a thing."

Which was when Norman turned puce and only just restrained himself from punching his soon-to-be ex-master on the nose.

"But," said Bruno, "If it's a knighthood you want, I'm sure I could see my way to talking to Missus Queen. Just so long as you *stay* with me."

And Norman was momentarily tempted. After all, the gig so far had been a good one. A lot of fun he'd had using his covert role in the shadows, skulking and lurking around the corridors of Parliament wearing a tatty old tracksuit while everyone else wore expensive suits. It was Norman's opportunity to dissimulate his superior intellect and simultaneously wave two fingers at the "little people" in both Westminster and the nation as a whole. Talk about powers behind thrones. But he also knew Junkett backwards, forwards, and inside out. How many false promises had he witnessed the guy making and breaking once he had got what he wanted? Zillions, that was how many. And should Norman now be so stupid as to fall for the knighthood that would never be? He didn't think so...far better to enjoy the public opprobrium hopefully produced by the left buttock shot. Everyone knew how draconian the Tory party could be when it came to replacing failed leaders. And in such circumstances, if Norman *were* to stick around, he would lose his job in any case and there would be *no* chance of either the knighthood or of anybody else in Parliament giving him a position of power, because nobody else in Parliament was as brain-dead or psychologically needy as Bruno.

"Norman, Norman, *puh-lease* don't go. I'll make you a knight, promise. Oh God, my *bott*om," Bruno whimpered in the background.

Which was when Norman experienced the epiphany in which he saw himself carving a whole new and different swathe through global political systems. What that would be beyond his cherished sloganeering populism, he had little more than an amorphous idea, but Norman hadn't built his career so far by sucking his thumb and wondering. A person of his talents would surely make his mark, and he was in no doubt it was far better to preempt events than allow them to overtake him. And if that meant No More Mister Nice Guy where the PM was concerned, bum blast wake-up call or no bum blast wake-up call, well amen to that.

Still dreaming of the yet more glorious international fame of the kind his American equivalent Sam Bundy had achieved, Norman therefore answered Bruno's mendacious special pleading by telling him go take a flying fuck at a rolling doughnut, a phrase for which his Eton and Oxford education had not fully prepared the PM.

"Pardon?" he said.

But by then Norman was through the door and out onto Downing Street, where he hurried past the assorted journos with the hood of his hoodie pulled down over his eyes while he unlocked his bike from the railings.

"Mister Gubbins, Mister Gubbins, any news about anything interesting?" the hacks chorused. But behind his back, Norman just flipped them the finger, climbed on his bike and pedalled off, leaving Bruno Junkett to lick his wounds. Not literally of course, although weaving his way around Trafalgar Square, Norman grinned at the novel image of Bruno for once trying to lick his own arse rather than everybody else's.

~ * ~

In Cambridge, Massachusetts, Sam Bundy was sipping whisky in the garden of his Harvard University 'special alumnus' home and feeling resentful, a not unusual feeling for Sam, despite the international acclaim he'd received for having invented the populist agenda that catapulted neo-fascists to power all around the world, most spectacularly Dougal Klank in America. He had even established populist academies in his name, including one at an 800-year-old monastery in Trisulti, south of Rome, but *still* there rankled the memory of Klank having fired him after only seven months into his role as chief advisor to the president on the grounds he'd lost his mind and learnt too late that "winning isn't as easy as I made it look."

"I...I...I and another goddam *I*," Sam muttered into his whisky. "'I' in every sentence. 'I' to the power on *n* and the exclusion of everybody else on the planet."

Okay, he'd had the guy figured for a sociopath from day one, but hadn't reckoned on the depths of his hubris. And nor was it any consolation to see replacement chief advisor after replacement chief advisor fired in Sam's wake. The more fool them, he concluded. If *he* hadn't intuited the full extent of the president's solipsism, how could they? What mattered to Sam above all now, however, was the son of a bitch shouldn't remain in the White House after the upcoming election later in the year. Maybe his asinine blanking of Covid-19 as a mere inconvenience would also contribute to *his* demise, never mind how often he changed the story to one that showed him in a better light—ironically in the very way Sam had taught him. Now, in the pursuit of Covid-19 denial, he had chosen to divert attention from the millions of non-event, but nonetheless embarrassing US deaths, by bullying China and playing the QAnon tough guy card by sending armed troops onto the streets of suburban America to counter the menace of "Satanist paedophiles" and in the same bag the "communist terrorists" who had emerged in the wake of the George Floyd murder and the Black Lives Matter protests.

"Asshole. God*dam* asshole," Sam was mumbling when his phone trilled its Wagnerian ringtone, the kind of which Hitler would have approved.

"Yeah, Norm. Long time no hear. Wassup?"

So Norman told him, and Sam spilled his whisky and almost fell off his chair laughing.

"Man, some neat trick," he managed to splutter when the laughing was over. "So now the creep's *truly* half-assed. You're a hero."

Norman preened at such praise from his long-time mentor. The pair had only met in person a couple of times at underground populist conferences, but Sam had taken a pointed interest in his acolyte's doings ever since Junkett's 2016 Brexit success, coming as it did only months before Klank's elevation to the White House. Seventeen years younger than him Norman might be, but clearly he was singing from the same hymn sheet and Sam had always been only too happy to be on the end of a line if there was any mileage in the conversation for *him.*

"Just a little idea I had," said Norman.

"And he knows it was you who did it?"

"No way. It was a monster mosquito he was blaming."

Sam shook his head. "Mosquitoes in the UK and in the *john*? This ain't Florida in summertime we're talking, Norm."

"He's not the most focused of people, Sam. You know that."

"You got that right. Anyways, you just called to tell me the story?"

Which was when Norman confessed to the nagging worry that having shot the PM in the left buttock, he might also have shot himself in the foot, because if Bruno were laughed out of town, his albeit ex-chief (and only) adviser Norman would be too and there would be no higher jobs for either of them to go to. Having been booted upstairs despite lies, crimes, and indiscretions all his charmed life, there was now no other more important position in the land for Junkett, bar king.

Sam laughed. "And last I heard that job's already occupied, right?"

"By a queen, as it happens, Sam. And the only way he's going to get rid of her is through another Cromwell-type revolution. But I don't reckon that has legs. Brits like being subjects in the royal pantomime, are proud of it even. It's all part of the sovereignty bullshit we peddled in the Brexit campaign. All we had to do was tell them being subjects of Johnny Foreigner Europeans instead of their blessed monarch would be living hell, and into the polling booths they flooded to vote Leave. You'll remember the Take Back Control line."

"I sure do and it worked pretty good. A little like our No Taxation Without Representation when we were getting free of your mad king George."

"Yeah, and look where you ended up two hundred and thirty-nine years down the line. For 'mad king George' read 'mad king Klank'."

"While all you got out of Brexit was jackass Junkett,"

"Correct."

"Which was how come you shot him in the ass."

"Also right. I go out of my way to get the dickhead elected PM and does he repay me? The fuck he does. Did Klank repay you?"

"The fuck he did. Fucking fired me."

"So where does that leave the two of us now, Sam?"

Bundy nodded. "A case of thanks for your contribution, guys, now take a hike."

"Exactly. No knighthood for me, and the heave-ho for you."

Hiatus while Sam poured himself a fresh whisky, rubbed his chin, and stared off.

"Sam, you still there?"

"I'm here."

"So what do we do about Klank and Junkett? Remember that line about power tending to corrupt, absolute power corrupting absolutely, and great men almost always being bad men?"

"That *your* line, Norm? Seems to me like I heard it someplace else before."

"Not mine. Some lord called Acton way back in some other century."

"And you figure I should follow your lead and shoot Klank in the ass, too?"

"It's an idea, Sam. Just...an...*idea*," said Norman. "Just keeping you up to speed, that's all. Get back to me when you've thought it through. After all that's happened to us recently, what we most need now is to stick together, help each other out. Maybe there's a whole new world out there for both of us."

"I hear you, buddy. Have a nice day now," said Sam, cutting the call, pouring himself another slug of whisky, and drinking to the day he never saw or heard from the klutz Gubbins again. Who gave a good goddam what happened to him or the UK? Living off its empire history was all the U-freaking-K was good at doing. Meanwhile, like Bruno Junkett, Sam had his own wounds to lick.

Such were the self-pitying concerns of meddlesome politicos like Norman Gubbins and Sam Bundy, but their angst was as nothing by comparison to the suffering being dispensed to the helpless masses by Monseigneur Coronavirus and the medicos destined to care for them.

Two

In Scotland, everybody had hated English Tories on principle for years, but for their current leader, Bruno Junkett, they reserved an abhorrence verging on the visceral. He was a persona *so* non grata the only way he could visit the country was to stay airborne as long as possible and touch down for no more than ten minutes per visit on the very remotest outskirts of the country, such as the Outer Hebrides, unless he wished to face insults and cabers tossed at him, thereby rendering the entire trip embarrassing, painful and pointless. The only person Scots despised more than Bruno Junkett was Dougal Klank, who owned a frequently picketed golf club in Balmedie, Aberdeenshire, and was also never allowed off his helicopter, *if* permitted to visit at all, for fear of emasculation, at the very least. The Scots are a proud people who don't tolerate fools at all, let alone gladly. It was no wonder so many of them had for so long harboured yearnings to free themselves forever from all involvement in the notion of a 'United' Kingdom. Okay, they had provided the Anglos with James VI & I, the only decent king they'd ever had, but that was all water under far too many bridges far too long ago.

It was on the Wednesday lunchtime following Bruno's most recent futile expedition over what was once Hadrian's Wall, in a vain attempt to forestall the latest burgeoning demands for Scottish independence after his government's stumbling attempts to handle Covid-19, that first minister Nigella Strachan and her husband, Neil, tuned into Prime Minister's Question Time down in the Westminster cesspit of a parliament. As usual, Bruno was being pressed for clarity by the cool and collected lawyerly Leader of the Opposition, ex-Director of Public Prosecutions, Sir Keith Staniford, on exactly *how* and on what timetable the prime minister was proposing to deal with folk affected by the next expected spike in coronavirus, to which, with no Norman Gubbins on hand to advise him, Bruno had no answer. Probably best not to reply, "Let them eat cake," he reckoned, but what *else* was he supposed to say? In a Commons chamber infested with social distancing and echoing emptiness, it wasn't even as if he could turn to his massed supporters on the backbenches for inspiration, because most of them were self-isolating—from Bruno, let alone coronavirus.

Incensed and wobbly on his feet, Bruno's riposte was therefore little more than a burbled, ratty yellow-dyed hair-tearing, lectern-thumping *ad hominem* diatribe aimed at Sir Keith, sitting cross-legged and eyebrow-raising on the Labour front bench opposite, suggesting the Opposition leader didn't know his arse from his elbow and it was high time he resigned unless he wanted Parliament pre-rogued for foul play again.

"Very helpful and thank you so much for the non-clarification, PM. And I assume it was to the twenty-nineteen '*pro*rogation' you were referring," said Sir Keith, as Bruno collapsed back onto his bench where, given his buttock issue, he had little choice but to tilt to the left and do his best to hold himself upright with an outstretched hand. But that sadly couldn't take the strain of so much obesity, causing Bruno to collapse sideways and then tumble to the floor, thereby giving rise to titters around the Chamber. In his Oxford days, Bruno would have tittered too, his favourite joke at the time defining "titters" as chaps who circled the Chamber tweaking lady members' nipples.

In Edinburgh, Nigella and Neil slapped their thighs and chortled. There was no sight more pleasing to them than a British Tory PM, especially Bruno Junkett, writhing about on the floor of the Commons.

"What d'ye think's the matter with him, Neil? Looks tae me like a bum issue," said Nigella, when the chortling was more or less over.

"The usual, pissed again?" Neil offered.

"Nae, it's something more structural in the downstairs department," said Nigella. "I need tae get to the bottom of this—so tae speak."

"Delve away, my dear, but whatever you find, be heartened by what we've just seen. It'll do our hopes of freedom nae damage at all."

"Aye, there is that tae it," Nigella agreed.

"Especially now, as under your leadership we're pretty much down tae zero on Covid deaths up here, while thanks tae Bruno, south of the border there are still new waves all over the place and coffins stacked up in the morgues. In my reckoning, his days in Downing Street are numbered in single figures."

Nigella thanked her husband for the compliment, but remained interested in the cause of Bruno's sudden prostration and took out her phone looking for answers. Not one to leave a stone unturned was Nigella Strachan, hence her success as first minister. And her searches of the conventional and social media, all of them hysterical with the story, were instantly rewarded with photos, blogs, speculation, opinions, and all the usual razzmatazz of early twenty-first century media life on planet Earth. The "fact" they were all basing their hysteria on was the one from a credible but unnamed source asserting Bruno had had half his bottom shot off by an underground Russian marksman on the Kremlin's orders for not performing as ordered after their support in his election as PM.

Norman Gubbins—the "unnamed source"—reckoned it an inspired further contribution to Junkett's downfall. As evinced by Klank's midnight usage of social media, there was nothing like a good cyber-bot to stir the pot.

In Moscow, however, President-for-Life-and-Beyond, Igor Ripyurpanzov, as usual denied any knowledge of such accusations, tweeting he had nothing to do with any of them—which was for once true, at least so far as the bottom blasting was concerned—and suggesting *if* such an outrage had occurred, it would probably have been the work of dissident ex-Soviet criminals. Meanwhile, he would expect soonest an apology from Downing Street, in the absence of which he would consider severing all diplomatic relations and declaring the UK a pariah state. No wonder he and Klank got on so famously with each other.

"Bugger," said Bruno, who'd been driven back the short distance from Parliament to Downing Street in a black Range Rover Sport with seats specially enhanced for the comfort of passengers with missing left buttocks. Having been stretchered upstairs to his private apartment, he was now spreadeagled on his curtained four-poster bed catching up with the news in his iPod, and not liking what he was seeing.

"Get Gubbins in here fastest. Bally what's-his-name ,the Foreign Sec, says we've got a problem with the Bolsheviks over my botty probs," he instructed his butler, Boris, who tried buzzing Norman several times, but without success.

"Sorry, sir, but Mister Gubbins appears not to be available."

"Not a*vailable*? Normally he's here the moment I call him," shrieked Bruno, who amongst other ailments also suffered from short-term memory loss attributed to either ADHD (Attention Deficit Hyperactivity Disorder) or EOD (Early Onset Dementia) by clinicians who were paid to keep their judgements to themselves or face disbarment. By the more cynical in the media, such lapses were seen as a deliberate pretence strategy, because there was nothing like conveniently forgetting one's frequent mistakes, drawing a line under them, highlighting some fictitious success story in their stead and moving on, again à la Klank. But this time, it was for real.

"Sorry sir, nothing I can do about it," said Boris. "Perhaps it's just a sign of the times."

"Sign of the *times*, Boris?"

"You know, sir, 'the new normal.' One hears the phrase in the media all the time."

In his white Winnebago parked in a Corvid-19 decimated mobile home park a few miles north of Penzance, Cornwall, Norman congratulated himself on having bugged the PM's private quarters for sound in his early days at Downing Street and smiled. The new norm*al*, eh? Well, look out for the new Norm*an*, Bruno past-your-sell-by-date Junkett.

~ * ~

Sam Bundy liked the idea of rendering Dougal Klank as obviously half-assed as Bruno Junkett but, as an independent thinker, wasn't minded to employ exactly the same method as Gubbins. Yes, it had been ingenious, but how was Sam to wheedle his way back into the White House and refit the presidential john when Klank had already given orders to have him shot on sight if he ever again tried to set foot across the threshold? You didn't ruffle this egomaniac's feathers and hope to get away with it. This was America, after all, where issues were traditionally resolved with Colt .45 bullets, not little washroom darts; ergo *shooting* off one of Klank's buttocks would be far more apposite than merely puncturing it. But there remained the problem of access. Klank never went anywhere without satellite camera supervision and flanked by armed sycophants, and he always wore body armour under his blue suit jackets, white shirts, and red ties. Bundy happened to know, however, he didn't wear it under his trousers, claiming it would restrict and therefore damage his prized manhood. Sooo, there was a window of opportunity, particularly as it was his ass that was the target and if he got his dick shot off, too, well that would be just a bonus.

But the problem of access remained. Nothing better would Sam have liked than to shoot the dork's privates off personally, but there was no way of achieving that. What he needed was a trusted guy on the inside of Klank's presidential machinery who would do the dirty deed for him, someone pretending the required quotidian obeisance, yet under the obsequious surface so deeply piqued by the lack of recognition coming his way he might be persuaded to take action. Sam could list sundry such riven interns from his White House days, because Klank never thanked or praised anyone for their ass kissing—it was expected, his just desserts for being the godlike boy king. No ass-kissing, and it was goodbye job. There was, however, *one* guy, actually a *gal*, who fitted the bill and Sam planned on contacting her just as soon as he could relocate her number. Okay, there could be the little problem of the affair between them that had gone badly south, but on the upside, she was the smartest woman he'd ever met and might just consider his request in the current circumstances of trying to halt Klank's re-election plans in their tracks. Aside from being smart, she was an A1 shooter with medals from the NRA. *Plus,* Sam knew Klank had tried three times to bed her and three times she'd told him she'd have his balls for breakfast if he laid a finger on her. Some woman, this Catya Rampersad, whose originally Trinidadian family were now long-time residents of New Orleans and justifiably proud of their daughter's prestigious post-Stanford Law School post on Capitol Hill. They didn't like the BAME Co-Ordinator title much, or its job description as token defender of Dougal Klank, to be wheeled out every time he was branded a White Supremacist exploiter of Black, Asian, and Minority Ethnic folk and to deny the claims as "Absurd Fake News." What they *did* like at these media scrums, though, was the way Catya would use the occasions, through a secret code of covert gestures and eye-swivelling known well to the brothers and sisters, to deconstruct as she was saying them the very words passing her lips. What they liked even better were the super-encrypted texts Catya would send them, explaining the anti-Klank strategies she was putting in place behind *very* closed doors on the days she wasn't bullshitting specially cloned journos from mainly Fox News.

"Yeah, Catya could be the gal," Sam mumbled to himself as he scrolled down the hundreds of 'favourites' numbers on his phone, hoping to hell he hadn't deleted it the day she had deleted him only a week after he'd be deleted by Klank.

It wasn't as though they'd got along badly with each other...far from it. No sex involved, but many long conversations into the night about the future of America. Until that awful pre-dawn morning when Catya had finally concluded Sam's populist agenda to be "fundamentally antithetical" to the multi-racial future she foresaw for her country.

"First off, you get white supremacist Klank elected," she accused. "But much more importantly, in the process you blindly ditch in one fell swoop the whole underpinning of the original Constitution by distorting the line that spoke to 'empowerment by the sovereign authority of the people.' The question is, Sam, *which* people? The likes of Klank and his fascists, or the likes of me, mine, and all the decent white folks who've been driven underground? Get back in touch when you've thought it through. Meanwhile, have a nice life."

And then to Sam's deep regret, she was gone.

Ah, but here it finally was, her number. Not the White House one, but the private one she'd given him before they stopped being friends. The question was: did Sam have the cojones to call it, especially given the history of recent years?

Three

Sir Keith Staniford didn't believe Norman's Russian bottom-blaster post any more than he ever believed anything he read on the social media, where any fool could claim the world was flat, porcupines made excellent sex partners, and drinking Dettol cured Covid-19, which was really only pneumonia anyway. After all his years as a human rights QC, then Director of Public Prosecutions, Sir Keith knew only too well the age-old prosecutor's tactic of dropping an unproven assertion into his opening remarks in the full knowledge the judge wouldn't allow it into the court's transcript without evidence—but *still* it had been heard and noted by the jury.

Such was Sir Keith's current concern with Twitterdom, plenty of emotive opinion but no facts to back it up. Instead, there was just inflammatory invective hidden behind prejudicial sloganeering. How else would Klank have been elected president, Brexit have been railroaded through, or Junkett risen to the dizzy heights of PM? No, no, Sir Keith knew the schtick, all right, and cursed its success on a daily basis, blaming mainly the Gubbinses and Bundy Svengalis of this world hiding in the shadows. But if Junkett hadn't been shot in the arse by a Russian marksman on Ripyurpanzov's orders, then what *had* caused his sudden slump to the left and then collapse onto the Commons' floor? Sir Keith was no friend of Bruno's ideologically, personally, or in any other way, but as one human being to another, he *was* interested to find out what had really happened to his opposite number. Such was his belief in the humanistic roots of socialism, and hence the call he put through to Bruno in search of an answer.

"Yes, what d'you want *now*?" said Bruno, taking the call on the specially dedicated PM/Leader of the Opposition line to which he was obliged to respond, despite Gubbins' advice not to. But Gubbins had disappeared, hadn't he?

"Just checking to see how you were, PM. Sorry about events in the House," said Sir Keith, with as much concern as he could muster. After all, who was to know if, after so much of Gubbins' tutelage, it hadn't been the PM himself who'd manufactured the Russian marksman narrative, thereby creating an imaginary enemy to divert public attention from his current dilly-dallying between the deaths of either people or the economy during the annoyingly ongoing Covid pandemic. Which was precisely the same card Klank was playing with his victimisation of China as either the knowing progenitor of the disease or using TikTok to spy on US citizens and gather their personal data. Change the story before the truth bit you in the ass—in Bruno's case, literally.

"Thanks," said Bruno noncommittally, wondering what game the bloke was up to now. Probably just a polite intro before more demands for clarity over lockdowns and furloughs and workers' rights and all that stuff.

"With respect, what I was specifically interested in was..." Sir Keith was saying in his annoyingly legalist fashion until he was interrupted by one of Bruno's strategic coughing fits. Blighter wanted every T crossed and every I dotted. He'd learn soon enough that such was *not* the way to climb the slippery ladder of politics, but the more fool him—a bally knight already. On the basis of *what*, Bruno wondered. It wasn't as if *he* had Churchillianly rescued his country from the clutches of the obnoxious Euros, was it? He was just some upstart lawyer who'd taken over the unelectable Labour Party from the

Trotskyist mudslinger who'd led it down the toilet in the last election. No wonder Bruno had finished up with an unassailable eighty-seat majority and become the darling of the Tories.

"Was *what*?" said Bruno, having strategically recovered from his coughing fit. "Look, I'm rather busy being PM at the moment and…"

"The question of your bottom," Sir Keith continued undeterred.

For an instant Bruno considered the reply "dirty devil," as given by a suspect in one of the *Carry On* movies in response to being asked by a police inspector for an account of his motions over the last twenty-four hours. But he reckoned Staniford wouldn't see the funny side. Staniford didn't see the funny side of *any*thing.

Instead he said, "What a*bout* my bottom?"

Sir Keith sighed inaudibly. "You will have read the story in all the papers, Prime Minister."

"Of course I have."

Which, unusually for Junkett, was partly true. Apart from scanning a few headlines himself every day, normally Bruno got Gubbins to search through the meat of all press reports and only read out to him carefully selected quotes from pals in Fleet Street saying how brilliant and witty he was. Only Gubbins appeared to have done a runner, so this time Bruno had been obliged to dig a little deeper all on his own to check what's-his-name the foreign secretary had been banging on about with bally Bolsheviks shooting him in the bum. And the headlines he had seen were no fun even to squint at: "Bruno Bottom Blasted By Reds," "Junkett Rear-Ended By Ripyurpanzov," and so on and so irritatingly forth. And the further imaginative column inches had been even worse. High time he abolished some of the papers, he had concluded.

"And your views as to their veracity, PM?" Sir Keith laboured on with the patience of Job. "Any evidence so far as to the truth of their claims? One assumes you will by now have MI5 *and* MI6 on the case."

Which, even if he *had* been shot in the bottom by a Ruskie, Bruno would certainly *not* have done, perchance, accidently while on the case, the sleuthy spy chappies at Thames House and Vauxhall Cross were to unearth any evidence of Ripyurpanzov's helpful participation in his elevation to the heights of No. 10 Downing Street.

"Of course, of *course*," Bruno nonetheless lied. "But they won't find anything."

"May one ask why not, PM?"

Which was when Bruno's fragile patience ran out and he told Sir Keith what he still believed to be the facts of the matter—themselves a moveable feast in the Junkett mindset.

"Because what *really* happened was I was stung on the bum by a mosquito while taking a dump, that's *all*," he said, in what he thought of in his most persuasively mellifluous tone.

Unsurprisingly, like Sam Bundy, Sir Keith remained unimpressed. "A mos*quito* bite, PM, in Downing Street in April?"

"Yes. A very *big*, super-sized, weatherproof mosquito."

"And that was what caused you to fall over in the Chamber?"

"Yes."

"Well, many commiserations, and I hope you and your bottom soon get better," said Sir Keith. "At least one now knows The Kremlin had no part to play in this unfortunate episode."

"Quite, epso*lutely*," said Bruno, cutting the call without thanking the Leader of the Opposition for his concern.

Listening to this exchange in his white Winnebago, Norman Gubbins stroked his chin and wondered. Okay, so Bruno had for once told what he thought of as the truth, but still Norman didn't like Staniford sniffing around looking for loopholes, not at all he didn't. Unlike all the other politicians Norman had come across over the years, this one appeared to be a genuine truth seeker without ulterior motives, and therefore a *very* difficult opponent to handle.

"Mmmm," said Norman, staring out over the Cornish seascape, and finding nothing appealing in it. No big fan of Nature was Norman Gubbins, particularly when it threw into the mix game changers like Covid-19 to screw up all the best-laid plans of mice and geniuses like him. Fickle, that's what he reckoned Nature to be. The argument that the pandemic might be Her revenge for centuries of accelerating rape, pillage, and despoliation as prosecuted by tree huggers and Extinction

Rebellion activists he, like his ex-boss and Dougal Klank, mocked as mumbo jumbo from the lips of a bunch of crazed leftie Internet conspirators.

Nonetheless, it was a matter of some concern to him that Staniford should now be on the trail of the *true* cause of the PM's rear end anguish and, as evinced by his disbelieving tone, wasn't about to buy into the monster mosquito response any more than he would the contention shit was blue. One of those benighted, grinding truth seekers, that was Keith Staniford QC for you, God damn him. The very *last* person Norman needed breathing down his neck just now.

"Mmm," Norman re-mused, but to little avail.

~ * ~

Checking on the caller before picking up, Catya Rampersad thought fifteen times about accepting the call, and by the time she came to the sixteenth, it had gone to message. Which was good because it gave her the space she needed to wonder:

a) What the hell Sam Bundy wanted after all this time,

and,

b) What*ever* it was, should she listen to it?

What his message said was, "Hi, Cat. Long time no see and figured it was time we touched base again. Little project I got in mind. You might like it. Call me."

Since he'd been given the boot by Klank, Catya had kept an eye on Sam's career as the progenitor of rampages through wobbly democratic regimes by third-rate power seekers, and scorned every second of it as "the sovereign authority of the people" again and again was reinvented as the populist revenge of the dispossessed against their liberal elite and overeducated masters. Ironical indeed she'd found it when she'd heard that, under the guidance of some dork acolyte called Gumbins, Bruno Junkett had employed such tactics to become Brit leader. A friend of the people who'd been educated at Eton and Oxford and probably couldn't tell an ordinary person from a kangaroo, yeah, well screw you, Bruno. Many Black guys or gals at Eton or Oxford, were there? And wasn't Bundy's own alma mater just about elite as a person could get? In Catya's eyes, the whole goddam deal had hypocrisy written all over it and it was high time the folk who'd fallen for it wised up.

In the end, however, curiosity got the better of her, hoping it wouldn't kill her in the way of her namesake feline friends.

"Hi, Cat. Thanks for getting back to me," said Sam, all cuddly and friendly.

But Catya wasn't going for that schmooze. "Keep it brief, Bundy. I am kinda busy with Klank screw-ups."

Which was true. Not by doing her official job defending Klank misspeaks, which were encouragingly legion, as his narcissist's mind began to crumble under the weight of criticism from many quarters, but covertly by drawing as much attention to them as she could. Particularly where BAME folks were catching the flak. She was also working hard behind the scenes to disabuse the Bible-belt Klank believers he was their new messiah. Opening their eyes, as he sanctimoniously clutched a Bible to his heart on TV, to his assertion his opponent in the upcoming election was a godless hypocrite, when he was known to be a professed Catholic. Advertising this was precisely the sort of gratuitous lie to be expected of an insane misogynist WASP whose only true god was Mammon. *Any*thing she could do to loosen Klank's hold on the White House she was doing. Clandestine praise she had lavished on the Twitter boss for banning the president's tweeted contributions to his own election campaign. Encouragement also went to the guy who had never given up on Klank's fraudulent non-tax returns and to the brave women who had come forward publicly to announce he had groped or otherwise sexually exploited them. Call it *schadenfreude*, call it what you want. Catya called it justice of the kind that could never be achieved so long as Klank was president. And okay, she had to use all manner of devious methods to spread her messages, but so far as she was concerned, in this case the ends fully justified the means.

Sam wasn't going with the "keep it brief" though, wanting to know how her folks were doing, how the job was going, how *she* was, if she was still out at the rifle range on weekends...the whole chummy bag of tricks.

Catya sighed. "All good," she replied to the first three items, but said nothing about the rifle range. What business was that of Bundy's? As to *his* welfare, she asked nothing, leaving Sam huffy and for once at a loss for words.

It was Catya who broke his silence. "Tell me about this project of yours and keep it short," she said.

Which was when, recovering from his huffiness, Bundy recounted the story of Norman Gubbins arranging for Bruno Junkett to be shot in the left buttock with a toilet dart. Obviously enough, Catya had read of the Brit PM's bottom problems and their attribution to Igor Ripyurpanzov, but this was the first time she'd heard the toilet angle to the story at which she laughed, couldn't help herself. Which encouraged Sam, who went on to explain how he had a similar fate in mind for Dougal Klank, only in true Wild West style i.e. with a few bullets in the ass instead of some dumb dart.

Which was when alert gongs started up in Catya's cerebral cortex. "You want *me* to shoot the creep in his ass?" she said, finally getting the rifle club enquiry.

"I'd do it myself, hon, only I can't get past the front gates, never mind into the house."

"Can I ask you one question, Bundy?"

"Shoot," said Sam, all fired up on gun issues.

"I can think of two reasons for you wanting me to shoot Klank in the ass. Reason one: you're still pissed at him for firing you. And reason two: you've finally seen the light with your goddam populism and are looking for a sacrificial president to offer up for your exculpation. So, which is it? I'd be very happy to think it was reason *numero due* but knowing you, I would go for reason *numero uno*," said Stanford Law School's top graduate of 2012. "So, which is it at play here? Your own skin or a final admission to the error of your ways?"

Which left Bundy just as dumbstruck as when she'd given him the push all those years ago with similar disapproval of a career he continued to think of as star studded.

"Well?" said Catya into the looming silence. "Cat got your tongue?"

More silence and then drone of a dead line so, irritated but also intrigued by the idea so long as it carried the right credentials, Catya hung up, too. Then she tapped in the number of her blues guitarist uncle, Silas Baudoin, who, after giving up on the American dream, had for the last twenty years lived alone except for a dog of indeterminate breed called Rufus in a cabin in a glade at the end of a creek leading off the Mississippi river just north of New Orleans. Whenever in doubt, Catya called Uncle Silas, now in his seventies and grizzled, but fit, spry, and probably more up to date on outside news than the average teen. Also a person armed and ready to defend his coastal forest swampland against any invader intent on its reinvention as a highway or the poaching of its native animals. Not by killing such a person, mind, but by scaring him shitless with pre-recorded screeches from the trees and carefully placed bullets as close as dammit to critical parts of the body such as heads. Childless himself, it was Uncle Silas who had taught his favourite niece how to handle a rifle.

Four

Before the elevation to his current prominence, the then unknighted Keith Staniford had been not only a dedicated human rights barrister but also a fair-to-middling right midfielder for a Sunday league soccer team called Somers Town Academicals, the Accies for short. Every week, never mind the pressures of the job, he would turn out for them at all sorts of park venues in all sorts of weather.

"A bloke can learn a lot from soccer," he told a press hack at the time. "Or from any team game, I suppose. The point is, it's never about the individual, it's all about the team. Put eleven expensive prima donnas out on the pitch and they'll never win anything. Put out eleven blokes who know and care for each other and operate as a *unit* and the chances of victory are significantly increased. It's the whole that matters, not the individual parts."

He went on to say that, next to his committed socialist upbringing in Yorkshire, soccer as he reckoned it should be played had been the biggest influence on his thinking. Which marked him out as pretty much the diametrical opposite of Eton and Oxford educated, Bullingdon Club playboy, Bruno Junkett. Or indeed Norman Gubbins, who was descended from landowners in County Durham and had also relished the laddish privileges of Oxford where, for the record, Keith Staniford had been a postgrad student, albeit one with a greater interest in his legal studies and college soccer than wenching and power grabbing. *Mens sana in corpore sano* were pretty much his bywords.

It was some days later, as he reflected on the unsatisfactory vacuity of his bottom issue conversation with Junkett, that Sir Keith's thought processes began seeking out more credible explanations for what was very evidently a somewhat more serious bottom injury than that which could ever have been caused by a "big, super-sized, weatherproof" mosquito. Just more off-the-cuff hyperbole from the mouth of an inveterate logorrhea sufferer, he concluded. But if not a monster mosquito, then what? Such was the question he was asking himself as, from apparently nowhere, came the insight that for several days around the Commons nothing had been seen of the creep Gubbins.

"Mmm," mused Sir Keith, wondering if there might be any connection between Bruno's lamentable incapacity to answer any question about *anything* in the House, never mind enquiries about his bottom, and the obvious absence of his chief and only adviser. After all, it was well known Junkett relied one hundred percent on Gubbins to provide the neurons his master was so signally short of, so...

That was when Sir Keith concluded that if he wanted a satisfactory explanation to this conundrum, it would be incumbent on him fastest to locate the whereabouts of the missing Gubbins, which he had no time to conduct in person. With this in mind, he called The Accies' one-time super-striker, George Ballentine, who'd retired from the game with knee ligament problems but still ran his Missing Persons/ PI outfit in Hackney. Sir Keith spoke to George on a regular basis, particularly to keep up on grass roots' responses to the Black Lives Matter movement to which he'd offered George free legal advice should it be needed.

"Yeah bro, how's it going?" said George.

"Good, and you?"

"It's going, better than that I can't say. This damn bug's causing all kinds of hassle. Any more restrictions, never mind another lockdown, and we're looking at more suicides and more domestic violence. Already loads of guys in the 'hood are out of work and doing runners 'cos they can't pay the bills and the kids're driving them crazy with home schooling. I get their ladies on the line day and night wanting me to find them, which I'd be only too happy to do if I had the staff. Only their furloughs won't last forever and I have no cash flow, so…"

Sir Keith nodded sadly. It was a similar story for small businesses across the land as Bruno Junkett and his 'government' dithered between economy-boosting "policies" one day and then put the brakes on them the next, if the infection rate increased, thus aiding neither business nor the Covid death rate in the long term. And who suffered most from these footling indecisions? The folk at the bottom, that's who, while the rich jumped at the opportunity to release themselves from the horrors of lockdown by taking government advice to holiday while they could, and jetting off to overseas destinations where they stood an excellent chance of either contracting Covid-19 and bringing it back home or passing it on to their hosts. Hence the later Covid spikes in both the UK and places like Italy, Greece and Spain, whose failing hospitality industries had been only too happy to drop their guard and welcome all comers.

"Sorry to hear that, George," said Sir Keith.

"I know you are. And that's not something I would say to just any bloke in your position. I still remember those forty-yard passes you sent up from midfield right to my feet. *You* were the guy who really scored all those goals for The Accies, Keith, not me."

"Oh, I don't know. You were the one with the killer instinct. The few times I got anywhere near goal, I'd fall over or whack the ball ten yards over the bar."

George laughed. *Sir* bloody Keith the bloke was now, but still you couldn't get him to own up to being any good at anything. Like every success he'd had was some sort of accident. George loved the guy.

"Anyhow, pal, reason for the call? Just the usual, or was it something special?" he asked.

That caused Sir Keith to hesitate. If George had no staff and no money, how could he be expected to track down PM-Whisperer

Gubbins who, incidentally, Sir Keith knew to be "earning" a six-figure salary. It wasn't as though he could use Party funds for the job, which was only a hunch and needed to be carried out *in camera*. Neither would he ask George for a freebie for old times' sake. Not part of Sir Keith's ethics at all. So, from his pocket the money would be have to be paid.

"You still there, Keith?" said George.

That was when the Leader of Her Majesty's Opposition confirmed he was and, on condition of total confidentiality, explained the background to the request he was about to make which, given its source, a gobsmacked George took seriously. As an avid news freak, he'd read all the social and normal media reports about Junkett's bum difficulties, none of which, like Sir Keith, he'd believed. But here was top-drawer lawyer and now the leader of his beloved Labour Party, suggesting there might be some connection between the PM's arse injury and the apparently now vanished person George loathed most on the planet after Junkett himself—and of course, Dougal Klank.

"You want me to find him, right?" he said.

"That was my hope. But of course, if it's too much to ask given your staffing problems, I'd perfectly understand, George. If you *were* to be willing, however, all bills would be sent to my private address."

"Man, I would do this for free. Close up shop for a while and get to it. The only thing you have to hope is the guy's still in one piece when I deliver him to you. Any bruising he might have around the eyes and nose and suchlike will have been the result of him banging his head on my dashboard because of a sudden change in the traffic lights, okay?"

"No broken limbs or anything like that, though, George. Preferably no damage at all."

"You got it, bro. Now gimme any details you've got to get me started."

So, Sir Keith confided all he knew of Norman's possible identifiers, which was little more than the probably fake email address and couple of equally unlikely throwdown mobile numbers circulating around Parliament. Of where the bloke lived there was no information, and any there was would in any case be hidden away in the bowels of 10

Downing Street and thus very obviously beyond the reach of even the CIA.

"Okay, not a lot to go on, but leave it to me," said George, who enjoyed a challenge as much as he liked scoring goals for the Accies. Plus, he was digitally mega savvy, which allowed him all manner of ways and means.

"You're a star, George."

"Save the praise till I bring him in, Keith. And hey, keep up the good work at PMQs. Any chance you get to raise Black Lives Matter or the Windrush deportations, let him have it with both barrels."

"It would be my pleasure, George. Now you take care."

"Yeah, yeah. And stay safe yourself, my friend."

~ * ~

All Silas Baudoin's days were the same. He and Rufus awoke with the sun, breakfasted meagrely on grits and suchlike, then, according to whim, either paddled down the creek in his pirogue to see how the big ol' Mississippi was coping with Covid-19—whether there were any more steamboats on the river yet—or roamed the local forest tracks to check out the well-being of the native flora and fauna. On all these trips, Silas always carried his old Winchester Model 1894 rifle in case he were to meet up with hunters of indigenous animals like black bears, skunks, possums and suchlike. Which sometimes he did, but they rarely came back after Silas had loosed off a couple of warning rounds into mid-air or, if they stood their ground, a few carefully targeted bullets into the ground they were standing on or the air just above their heads. That's how his and Rufus's mornings were spent.

Then there was a vegan lunch consisting of plants and fruits offered by the forest, which Silas would cook up into tasty dishes to which even Rufus had become accustomed. Being a dog, in the early days he'd protested, preferring meaty dishes but, after having rescued the creature from the clutches of an otter hunter called Mad Mungo, Silas had told him it was either this or nothing, buddy. And Rufus had converted quickly to the vegan menu, especially when he learned how carefully Silas selected his plants and fruits, making sure they and their offspring would all live to see another day. Not just to feed him and Rufus, but because that was their right, just as it was the right of cows, chickens, fish, and suchlike not to end up on humans' dinner plates. Then, of course, there was the planet to save from over-farming.

In the afternoon, sitting out on the porch of the little cabin he had built himself from carefully cut timber from forest water oaks, with Rufus lying at his feet, Silas would play his guitar for an hour or two, knocking out numbers by favourites such as Robert Johnson, John Lee Hooker and Big Bill Broonzy, but also making up his own songs about the world as he'd seen it over seventy years and some. There were paeans to nature and the animals he sought to protect, of course there were. But there were also bitter songs about the way nothing had truly changed over the decades for the Black folks, despite Martin Luther King Jr. and Barack Obama, *vide* the recent murder of George Floyd. A big supporter of Black Lives Matter was Silas Baudoin, who, despite his isolation, kept up with the news on the smartphone gifted him by his beloved niece Catya and kept in shape by his local New Orleans nephew, Matthias. When the guitar playing was over, he would spend another hour or so checking through Covid-19 and other developments across the globe, his fury mainly focusing on Dougal Klank. His newest song was called "Nice Hair Doug," derived from the presidential decree for more powerful shower head nozzles so his hair could always turn out "perfect." The lyrics are too obscene for inclusion in this narrative.

Then it would be time for the evening cook-up, accompanied by a glass or four of home brewed muscadine grape wine, which by sundown would have him ready for the bed in which he slept the sleep of the just until the following morning when the routine began all over again.

By twenty-first century, itchy, twitchy, international tourist standards, such a life would doubtless be thought terminally tedious, but not to Silas who, if ever challenged on the issue—which he wasn't— would have replied, "Variety may be the spice of life, but repetition is its essence," a notion he would have been happy to justify with reference to any number of philosophical texts in French, German and

English that lined the shelves of his hut's only bedroom. If the word 'autodidact' hadn't already existed, it would have had to be invented to describe Silas Baudoin.

It was in phase two of such a day, while working on "Nice Hair Doug" and struggling with a half-decent rhyme for 'asshole' that his phone took to playing its Johnny B. Goode ringtone, which stopped Silas in his tracks.

"Goddam," he said, laying the battered old Gibson to one side while fumbling in the pockets of his dungarees. Still, it had to be a family member because nobody else ever called him, so it was a case of "act nice, Silas"—even with the downtown kinfolk who made no secret of the fact they thought he was nuts.

"Hold on, I'm coming," he said, prodding at the screen in an effort to remember how to accept calls.

And then he had it, the little green dealie that flashed ACCEPT CALL.

"Uncle Silas?" said Catya.

"Honey, so great hearing from you!" said Silas and meaning it. A gal after his own heart was Catya. "You calling about the news?"

"News?" his beloved niece was saying when, as sometimes happened when calling Uncle Silas, the line went dead.

<h1 style="text-align:center">*Five*</h1>

At the White House, Dougal Klank was lying back in his barber's chair getting his hair washed and rinsed by his coiffeuse, Margot Komova (not her real name), with the new super-powerful showerhead nozzle that wasted more water than the average car wash facility on limo day. Next would come the blond rinse, careful combing, quiff styling, and sticking down of flyaway bits as he admired himself in the mirror, like Narcissus in his pool.

"Looking pretty good for a guy my age, huh Margot?" he said, which produced only silence from Margot, who wasn't playing the nymph Echo's role in the ancient myth, far from it. Every time he reached around behind him to squeeze her ass, she would slap the groping hand and tell him the next time he tried that he could go find himself a new coiffeuse.

"Playing hard to get, huh honeypie?" said Klank.

"No, just doing my job...Mister President."

That was how Klank insisted on being addressed at all times by all members of his staff. Otherwise, they got fired or stiffed.

"Yeah, yeah. And who pays your wages, honey?"

"The American taxpayer."

"Tell *that* to the Marines, sweetheart," said Klank, reaching down to unzip his pants and wiggling his ass about. "*I* get what *I* pay for."

Which was when Margot Komova switched on the overhead hair drier to top heat and full blast, thereby singeing Klank's hair and blowing it in many different directions, causing him to shriek and clutch at his head while she headed to the door for what she then reckoned would be the last time.

"What's all the noise in there?" asked Hank O'Henry, as Margot slammed the door behind her.

Hank was Klank's personal assistant, who was also responsible for ensuring no untested and Covid-19 cleared visitor was ever allowed anywhere near the president, who publicly declared the virus to be no more dangerous than flu.

"Just the hair dryer doing what it's supposed to do...drying hair. It'll close down in a minute," said Komova (not her real name).

"Uh, huh. And ain't it *your* job to do that?"

"Hank, do me a favour, willya?"

"Sure, name it."

"Imagine you're me. Like *you*'re a woman hairdresser and the guy you're working on keeps trying to grab your ass, then gets his dick out. Would *you* switch off the machinery or would you leave it on to fry his hair a little and take a hike outta there?"

Hank shrugged and placed a cautionary forefinger across his lips. Imagining himself a woman hairdresser was a tough enough ask, but then, as he went on to indicate with what he hoped would be interpreted as a knowing wink, there was the extra difficulty of being seen or heard to be disobeying Klank's orders, for there was super-tight security everywhere in his vicinity.

"Silence the best you can come up with, O'Henry?" said Margot failing to interpret either the lip deal or the wink.

Hank shrugged some more then, finger-hooking Margot out of range of the hidden microphones and CCTV cameras, walked her to the White House rear entrance. In the interests of a watertight cover story, along the way he explained to the super security system how "the poor guy" had been under a lot of pressure.

"Only yesterday he was accused by some leftist false news guy at a press conference of telling over twenty thousand lies since he became pres. Imagine how that would make *you* feel. Edgy right? Angry even," he continued dutifully, until they finally neared the exit and the fresh air beyond.

Margot shook her head. "Which is his excuse for pulling his cock out while getting his hair done? Maybe you can't see it, Hank, but the guy's a sicko nut job. Now show me the way out of this hell hole before I run back in there and do something I promise I won't regret."

It wasn't until the two of them were out in the grassy gardens beneath a couple of unbugged American Chestnuts that Hank dropped the mask of Klank servitude.

"And I wouldn't blame you, but now's not the time," he said.

"I thought you were defending him, his personal bodyguard or whatever."

"Yeah, well I need to cover my back, right? Truth is, I'm with you on the sicko nut job idea. Just waiting my moment is all."

"To do what?"

Hank shrugged. "Right now I don't know. But listen, Margot, I'm on your side on this. Look, you ever get serious about doing the freak serious harm," he said, slipping a sealed envelope into her hand, "you just give me a call. Meantime you take care and stay safe, okay?"

"Sure, okay. And you, too," said Margot as Hank turned and headed back to what in his head he now thought of as the Hell House.

Once outside on Pennsylvania Avenue, Margot opened the envelope, checked its contents, raised her eyebrows, and called the only other White House insider she exchanged occasional helloes with...Catya Rampersad.

~ * ~

Bored with Cornwall, fearful he might catch Covid-19 from the sudden influx of staycationers to the place, and most of all twitchy and crotchety at the self-inflicted absence of his Westminster power addiction, Norman Gubbins drove his Winnebago back to the rented basement rooms in Kentish Town, London, where he went on weekdays to escape the exigencies of family life at the address occupied by his wife and small son. All along the way, he punished himself, wondering if he'd done the right thing by shooting Bruno Junkett in the left buttock, then stomping off in a hissy fit. All the prat had needed to do was recommend him for a knighthood, for God's sake, and none of this would have been necessary. Still, no good crying over spilt sperm, as his father used to say. It is what it is, end of story.

Absorbed as he was by such thoughts when he drew up outside the house in Bartholomew Road, he paid no attention to the Black bloke fiddling with his phone on the pavement opposite. It was only when George Ballentine strolled across the street and asked if he might have a little chat that Norman, in true Norman style, told him to fuck off... he didn't give money to homeless beggars because they only spent it on drugs.

And how, you will be wondering, had George located Norman so easily? Through the wonders of modern technology, that was how—by hacking into the possibly throwdown phone numbers Sir Keith had given him, finding them not to be fake, and tracing the hiring of the Winnebago to a garage in Tottenham. Thereafter it had been a stroll in the park. Simply a matter of posing as a policeman requiring the licence plate number and Satnav details of the vehicle on the excuse it was suspected of having once been used in a bank robbery, and hey presto. Thereafter, all George had needed to do was sit at home, hack into the Satnav and track Norman's routes and destinations. It would have been something of a pain in the arse to have had to go to Cornwall to collect him, but then mercifully the guy was suddenly back on the M4 heading east to his power hub as Sir Keith had told George he suspected he might.

"I'm not homeless, I'm not a beggar, and I'm not an addict. I just wanted a moment of your time," said George, at which the ex-PM-Whisperer shrank back, held out a warning palm, and said if George didn't socially distance himself immediately, the police would be called.

"Yeah, yeah, another Black guy for them to suss and diss. Probably a Covid carrier, too 'cos of the colour of his skin."

"Don't come that crap with me, just fuck off like I told you," said Norman, who, as it happened, had been responsible for encouraging Bruno Junkett to ignore the BLM and BAME agendas altogether and leave police commanders to get on with their legitimate business of busting Blacks for any offence they could think of. Which advice Bruno had been only too happy to accept. Nothing like passing the buck and turning a deaf ear to irritating problems, until one way or another they went away of their own accord. No blame, no pain.

"And you would have said the same to a white guy who asked for a moment of your time?" said George, relaxing into his sadly familiar routine. "Maybe to ask you the way to the tube station or to comment on the pleasures of the neighbourhood because he was thinking of buying a place here? Like the house next door to yours, for example. I think not. Spoken by a Black guy 'Hi, there, I'm your new neighbour' are the six most feared words in the English language, right?"

From Norman's perspective, tired though he was after the horrors of Cornwall and the long drive back fretting over his self-imposed loss of Westminster power, it would have served him a lot better at this point simply to succumb to a reasonable assessment of the situation, apologize for his foolishness, and invite George in for a cup of coffee to take the sting out of the situation. But given his Nazi class attitudes, exacerbated as they were from the stress of the recent past, Norman was in no mood for such chivalric politesse.

"Just fuck the fuck *off*," he said instead, balling his hands into the sorts of fists that wouldn't have made an impression on a wet newspaper, then prodding one of them in the direction of his persecutor's nose.

Which stretched George's patience to a point 0.005% from its limits. How sweet it would have been to knock Norman to the ground—a feat easily achievable with a left hook to the jaw—and then to kneel on his neck in the manner of George Floyd's killer. But, employing every last iota of *sang froid*, yoga breathing deeply from the lower abdomen, sucking in his cheeks, grinding his teeth, and recalling Sir Keith's plea not to deliver Gubbins as a hospital case, he just about managed to take the diplomatic route.

"Not a good idea, pal," he said, ducking, catching Norman's fist en route to his nose and squeezing sufficiently to tame Norman but not to break any bones. "Not a good idea at *all*."

"Aaaaaaaaggghhh," shrieked Norman hyperbolically, because never before had he been on the receiving end of rough treatment of any kind. Never played physical contact sports or indeed any sports at all, his body being what he thought of as a temple. Wimp would be the best way of thinking about Norman Gubbins. That was certainly how ace soccer striker George Ballentine thought of him at that moment. He thought even worse things when Norman went on to call him a Black bastard, but *still* somehow maintained his cool.

"Think Zen, George. Think Zen, Ohm, Ohm," he muttered to himself as he released Norman's hand and allowed its owner to flap it about while still hollering fit to bust.

George hoped there were no elderly self-isolating neighbours peering through their chintz-curtained windows in adjacent houses, or else he could have a Covid-19-inspired old folks riot on his hands. And whom would they blame for the kerfuffle? The Black guy, that was who. But mercifully, all was quiet on the Bartholomew Road front.

"Mister Gubbins," he said. "How about you calm down now? You tried to hit me and I caught your hand, but no damage done, right? I am prepared to forget you called me a Black bastard. *Now*, do you want to hear the reason I am here or don't you?"

Still flapping his hand about, Norman stared. "*Reason?*" he said.

Which was when George explained the nature of his mission and the interests of his friend and employer.

"That socialist toe-rag *Stani*ford?" Norman expostulated when the explanation was over.

"The same."

"Why the hell should I agree to speak to *him*?"

"Something to do with the PM's bottom. Not sure what, exactly. Look, why don't we let bygones be bygones and be grownups about this? Option one: like I said, I forget you called me a Black bastard and take you in one piece to meet Sir Keith. Or option two, you go on yabbering and being difficult, in which case you'll still meet Sir Keith, only in a lot of pain," said George, flexing the knuckles of his (big) right fist.

That was when, unsurprisingly given his "body as a temple" idea, Norman grunted, lowered his head but, muttering darkly but quietly, nonetheless accompanied George to his parked SUV.

Six

By the time Catya Rampersad finally got back through to her uncle, albeit on a crackly but otherwise secure line, she *had* heard the news Silas had cited, that of Sam Bundy's arrest, and she was delighted by it. Given the upcoming election, Klank's increasingly erratic behaviour, and the assurance of a Black woman for VP on the Democrats' election ticket, could the tide finally be turning?

"You knew the guy, huh?" said Silas.

"Briefly," Catya admitted. "By the time I arrived at the White House, he was already history and packing his bags. But yes."

"An asshole, huh?"

"The biggest, if you believe in American democracy, and I know you do."

"What's left of it after Klank," Silas grunted.

"Raaf, raaf," said Rufus.

"Precisely. One more term for that cocksucker, and what we're looking at is dictatorship. All of which was originally engineered by Bundy. Now he's looking at twenty years in the hole, and hooray for that."

"Remind me for what, honey."

"Taking millions of dollars from a phoney non-profit company called We Build The Wall…"

"Klank's Mexican wall?"

"Right."

"And you figure Klank knew about that?"

"He must have. Right now, he's denying any knowledge."

"Same old."

"Tell me about it."

"Raaf, *raaf*," said Rufus.

"Ookay, so at least one bad guy bites the dust."

"With luck, all the Republican shit kickers who were also on board for the scam. *If* Klank doesn't find some way of stiffing the Manhattan prosecutors ahead of the trial," said Catya.

"You know what, darlin'? I am soo glad to be living up my creek. Might sound crazy to you, might sound yellow-bellied, but I just don't know how you survive up there in the Washington swamp."

"Be honest with you, Uncle Silas, neither do I. It ain't easy getting up in the morning knowing what I know. But if *nobody* gets to report back from the front line, then who's to know how the war's going?"

"I love you, sweetheart."

"And I love you too, Uncle Silas. Still got your old Winchester working?"

"Excuse me?"

But the line went down again before Catya could explain the potential plans she had for her uncle and his gun.

~ * ~

In his private Downing Street office, Bruno Junkett was mooning about like the jilted lover he had so often been. Speaking to nobody, taking no calls, munching junk food from his fridge and quaffing chilled prosecco while the country teetered on the brink of health, educational, and economic crises one after the other, and the press became increasingly tetchy faced with daily back-of-a-cigarette-packet excuses and U-turns from junior ministers thoroughly pissed off at their boss's refusal to carry the can.

"Come Out, Come Out Wherever You Are" and "Anyone Seen The PM?" pretty much summoned up Fleet Street editors' refusal to believe in Junkett's post-Covid "minor indisposition," the smokescreen Number 10 had erected in defence of his absence. Not that Bruno gave two hoots what the press said. Dismissed them all as footling pish. *Far* more concerned was he that Norman Gubbins should return to his master ASAP because, having no ideas of his own, how else would he be able to run a country? And all this just because of some minor disagreement about something or another, exactly *what* Bruno couldn't remember. He had paid the ungrateful brainbox whore well enough, hadn't he?

And so matters had continued for the better part of the ten days after Gubbins flounced out to make his fortune elsewhere. Okay, the pains where the Bruno's fully functional left buttock once was had more or less subsided, although of course he kept falling off chairs not designed for the derrière-challenged, which wasn't much consolation. All in all, this was pretty much the lowest ebb Bruno could remember in his erstwhile silver-spoon-in-the-mouth life and career. Even his brief tussle with coronavirus had been better. At least then he'd been able to emerge from hospital after a brief stay heroically claiming he'd diced with death but had defeated the bug and was now brimming over with antibodies.

Then, late one evening, after downing a bottle and a third of prosecco, he had a brainwave, or at least what Bruno thought of as a brainwave, namely to declare Gubbins a missing person and get the experts on the job. Not that Scotland Yard's boss warmed to the idea, given the lack of support Bruno had given her officers when it came to policing the early days of the government's lockdown policy. In Germany and even Italy, such supervision had been carried out by the police and army and had been effective, but in Conservative freedom-loving England, Bruno left it all down to the renowned "British common sense" to follow the rules and do the right thing, which of course the also renownedly arrogant British didn't. Not enough hand washing did they do, hardly any masks did they wear, in groups of more than six they congregated all the time indoors and outdoors, apparently oblivious to the danger they were in. Hence the overstretched National Health Service and the hundred and twenty-five thousand odd deaths chalked up by the New Year, which ranked the UK close to the highest in the world. Not that Junkett seemed to notice or care, just went on blethering about lights at ends of tunnels in his occasional "I am the new Winston Churchill" addresses to the nation.

"We all have to pull together in this. just like we did in the Blitz," he announced at one of these Zoomed press events, conveniently ignoring the inaccuracy of the "we," seeing as he hadn't been born until well after WW2.

Still, albeit no admirer of Junkett—quite the opposite—and through grinding teeth, chief cop Crissie Richards had curmudgeonly agreed to lend a hand.

"Just give me the name, a photograph, and any online references you've got, and I'll see what I can do," she said.

At which Bruno became effusive with thanks, praise, and offers of police pay rises. But by then, Crissie had already cut the call. Just as well, because it spared Bruno the embarrassment of overhearing himself described by Crissie to her PA, Lucy Bellweather, as a "sad little mealy-mouthed tosser who could use a nappy change."

Try half-heartedly though the coppers did, however, it was far too late for Norman to be found at his Kentish Town basement, or indeed at his family home, and returned to his master, because by then George Ballentine had already driven him to the secret address in Chelsea Sir Keith Staniford kept for the sole purpose of keeping *his* family well away from any media spotlights.

Back Bruno therefore went to abject self-pity, appearing in public as little as possible and delegating to underlings from his cabinet stand-in roles in the Commons so they could take the flak from Keith Staniford for a change. And if they metaphorically fell on their arses, well *tant pis*—or "auntie pisses" as Bruno wittily translated the French for his own amusement, if nobody else's. At least the focus of criticism would be temporarily lifted from *him.* Meanwhile, he would take a little holiday in the Scottish Highlands, where he hoped nobody would recognize him, his live-in-lover/fiancée, or their baby.

Although of course, canny Scots instantly *did* and made sure they snapped the photos to back their sightings. Hence the very brief duration of the staycation and, on his hurried return to Downing Street, the flurry of media pieces pointing out the flagrant breach of his very own coronavirus anti-travel rules outside designated areas. "Another case of the rich getting the pleasure, while the poor get the disease," claimed *The Daily Snitch*, for example.

But, spurred into reaction by such "scurrilous reportage," Bruno eventually managed to stir himself from his Gubbins-lack chagrin, to change the story as he had been doing since he was at school, and to fight back with the announcement that pretty soon there would be a vaccine on the market that would put a stop to further infection "for once and for all."

Well, that had folk across the land sitting up and listening.

~ * ~

Released on a $5 million bond, a furious Sam Bundy was swinging his fists and rhetoric in all directions to prove not only his innocence but also the palpable guilt of the slimeball anti-American leftist group that had conspired in a "political hit job" to seek his arrest. There he was still spouting the same fear of "the other" sloganeering that had turned Americans against the Democrats in 2016 and inspired Norman Gubbins and Bruno Junkett to their Brexit victory in the same year. Fox News presenters were delighted and threw their weight in behind him. Which was all well and good, but what Sam really needed was support from the president he had helped win the White House. Only all Klank could say when interviewed was he felt very badly about the arrest, and hadn't been dealing with Bundy for a *very* long period of time. Also, he didn't know anything about the Build Me A Wall project, but didn't like the sound of it and figured Bundy had just been doing whatever it was for showboating reasons anyway.

"Fuck you *twice*," Sam hissed at the TV screen as he watched the usual mishmash of Klankish unreason. "Once for firing me and twice for not helping out in my hour of need. Man, do you have it coming."

His mood wasn't improved by calling Catya Rampersad to see if she'd made any progress with the idea he'd had for halving Krank's ass in the manner of Bruno Junkett's, and being told she hoped he got the maximum term of twenty years, unless of course he had the good luck to be hit by a meteorite meanwhile.

"If you think I'm going to do your dirty work for you, buster, you've got another think coming. You were always an asshole and so you shall remain," she told him, which did little to improve Sam's novel experience of ground zero self-esteem.

"Bitch," he muttered.

"You better believe it, Bundy. Wait and watch. Meantime, have a nice life. Or better still...don't."

Then the line went dead and, bereft of allies, Sam sank into a gloom not dissimilar to Bruno Junkett's, but without the benefit of power to sustain him, the international populist influence he had once so enjoyed now apparently on its way to being flushed down the S-bend.

~ * ~

Hearing the account of her recent dealings with Klank and Hank O'Henry from Margot Komova (real name Maggie McKenzie) on the phone from Pennsylvania Avenue, Catya had both commiserated with her and congratulated her.

"Poor you, but well done for standing up for yourself. Hope you set fire to what he laughingly calls his brain, too," she said.

"*Brain*? Are you kidding me? If the creep thinks at all, it's with what's left of his dick."

"Which everybody knows but won't say, in case they get stiffed. Margot, how about we meet up for a longer conversation? There's a Starbucks at 1730 Penn Ave, would that suit? Maybe tomorrow around noon?"

"Yeah, that would be great. I don't have a very full diary these days. The freaking Covid took that away."

"Even though you're the president's coiffeuse?"

"Even if I wear a face mask, a visor and surgical gloves, folks don't want me in their homes and I can understand that. While Klank looks any which way, pretends Covid isn't happening and will just go away of its own accord, takes no action, and talks up the busted economy instead, you know how many people have died across this country so far?"

"Going on a hundred thousand."

"That would be about right. But, hey, let's talk again tomorrow. It's been a long time since I had me a cappuccino, even if it's only a takeaway."

~ * ~

It *was* only takeaways they shared the following midday, but at least Catya and Maggie—both masked for health *and* political reasons—were able to find a table outside the Starbucks and, only ever having greeted each other *en passant* in the White House's corridors, get to know each other a little better. Which caused them some amusement when they checked each other more intimately. Both young and striking in their own way, but Catya a dusky mid-brown going on black, while Maggie was a natural blonde of the kind that might be expected on a Californian beach, even though she hailed originally from the Bronx. They'd known from their different accents where they both came from, but that was the size of it, so initially there was girly discussion of hair products, cosmetics, all that kind of stuff before any foray into more serious issues. Also, there was the shared admission they both liked a cigarette with their coffee.

"You figure we could get arrested?" said Maggie, looking this way and that along the sidewalk as she tweaked from her purse a pack of Marlboros.

Catya laughed. "You think I could give a good goddam with Covid coming at us around every corner? My idea is tobacco is a better bug beater than drinking detergent like Our Great Leader says. To my mind, the bug is terrified of catching cancer and flies off in a hurry."

Maggie chuckled at that and offered one of her Marlboros.

"Thanks honey," said Catya, "but I'm a Pall Mall person. Down south we go for the real McCoy."

And so it was that, to the amused approval of the Starbucks' baristas looking through their double-glazed window, the two women dropped their masks to their chins, sipped at their drinks, lit up, and smoked for America. It wasn't until after their second cappuccino and further Pall Malls and Marlboros they got down to finding out about each other's lives and then the shared reasons for which they both longed for Klank's comeuppance, preferably one in which he is hanged by the ankles from a tree in the White House gardens while the Black folks he'd ignored and the white women he'd raped took pot shots at him. To trim a labyrinthine story to its essence, this was also the moment, as yet unbeknownst to them, that Catya Rampersad and Maggie McKenzie fell in love with each other. Maybe it was the enduring albeit slowly changing legacy of hostility to same-sex relationships in America that initially blinded them to the *je ne sais quoi* feelings they experienced. Or maybe it was simple shyness, who knows? But it was over two more Starbucks cappuccinos and three more cigarettes each that the as yet covert seeds of infatuation were sown and would before too long blossom, strengthened as time passed by their delight at defying Klank's well-advertised disgust at even the notion of LGBTQ+ relationships, let alone those between guys, gals and transes of different ethnic origins. Grabbing women's pussies was A-OK, to be recommended, in fact. Kissing or groping a person of one's own gender, particularly a Black one, was *not*. The Bible said so. But, much more importantly, so did Dougal Klank. And then there were all the other shared reasons—too numerous to list here—for which Catya and Maggie had become ashamed to be American with Klank in the White House, which was a solid enough base for any two people to start sharing feelings for each other.

Upon parting to go their separate ways for the time being, there were promises to keep in touch and fleeting sisterly pecks on the cheek that no one, including Catya and Maggie, would have mistaken for the passions further down life's winding road. Such are the mysteries of the human condition.

Seven

To ensure his passenger stayed put during the crosstown crawl to Sir Keith Staniford's hideaway flat in Chelsea, George Ballentine employed a specially reinforced rear seat belt to dissuade Norman Gubbins from all but necessary movement, let alone the temptation to whack him over the head, cause a crash, and in the mayhem do a runner. That didn't stop Norman from *sotto voce* muttering, though. Mutter, mutter, mutter he went, all the way, mainly about the hugely successful role he'd played in putting the 'great' back into Great Britain, much in line with Klank's making America great again MAGA. About the axial part he'd played in the Brexit vote, about the hugely successful contribution he'd made to curbing immigration, about his cunning manipulation of the "little people" in both Parliament and the electorate, and about his efforts to cull the Covid-ridden BAME and Black Lives Matter males before they had a chance to infect the entire white population.

On the assumption all this muffled muttering meant either Gubbins had finally twigged as to why he'd been lifted from Bartholomew Avenue and was rehearsing the things he would say to Sir Keith to impress him, or that he had gone bananas at the prospect,

George kept his cool all the way to Marble Arch. But then Norman took to repeating the BLM male aspect of his muttering, and George *lost* his cool big time. Negotiating London traffic, which appeared to have doubled since bug-fearful folk had abandoned public transport, was bad enough, but half-hearing the neo-Nazi in the back was one bridge far too far.

"Shut the fuck *up*, dickhead, or I am going to pull over and help you eat your own balls," he yelled over his shoulder, the wise response to which would have been an apology and silence. But Norman hadn't been trained in the school of humble pie eating, especially not where Black people were concerned, so, as the traffic lights on Park Lane turned to green and George had no choice but to hit the accelerator, he continued with the summation of not only his excellent past achievements, but also his aims for the future. In addition to the castration of Covid-stricken Black males, these included the abolition of Parliament, the cessation of *all* forms of immigration, the shooting of asylum seekers crossing the Channel in dinghies, and the forced repatriation of any European still daring to live in the UK after Brexit. It was a pretty radical agenda of which Sam Bundy would have been proud. A shame he was temporarily out of circulation, but Norman was sure Klank would sort out *that* little problem with a presidential pardon.

On and on and *on* he chuntered along these lines until a fuming George negotiated his way to a side street opposite Harrods, where he skidded to a halt, climbed into the back seat and hit Norman so hard in the stomach he went "Oooooofffff" before doubling over and lolling at his restraints.

"That's it, pal, get a good look at where your dick is just in case next time you want to use it you lose it," said George, slamming the door and climbing back behind the wheel.

Despite his original promise to deliver Norman in one piece, George reckoned Sir Keith would understand the extremities to which his patience had been stretched before being forced to react. After all, how many times on the soccer pitch did a person have to suffer illegal tackles, whispered racist slurs, hair pulling and worse when the ref wasn't looking? Legion, that was how many. But then there was that satisfying moment in the shower room after the game when the whitey culprits would find themselves suddenly being kneed in the knackers while attached naked to coat hooks by their towels. Not once had George witnessed Sir Keith protest at such treatment. Normally he just looked the other way and grinned.

~ * ~

As a lifelong anti-theist, Silas Baudoin rarely played gospel songs, but shortly before Catya finally got back to him on a better line, he was fingerpicking his way through Louis Armstrong's version of "Nobody Knows the Trouble I've Seen." Which was a pretty apposite description of Silas's life, hence the move he'd never for a moment regretted, the one that took him away for ever from what paraded as civilisation. And yet the media were telling him the same crap was still going down. First George Floyd murdered, now Jacob Blake shot in the back by police at close range on the excuse they suspected him of carrying a knife.

"Maybe he was a gardener or a carpenter," Silas mused.

And what was Klank going to do about it? Sweet FA except send in the troops to stop the protest riots in Kenosha, Wisconsin, so the "shooting" could be stopped before the "looting" started. In his book, the paralysis Blake suffered after the gunshot wounds was nothing more than a useful campaign boost to his "save the suburbs" slogan to win over erstwhile lily-livered Democrat voters to his sad side.

"Same shit, different day," a furious Silas was muttering as Catya's call came through.

"Sorry for the delay, Uncle Silas," she said. "I've been kinda busy."

"No problemo, darlin', no problemo at all," said Silas again, carefully laying the old Gibson to one side. "Last I heard, you were asking if I still had my Winchester working."

"Some memory you've got, Uncle Silas."

"Yeah, only it's getting real selective. Times are I remember too *much*, mainly from the long ago. Other times I don't remember what I did yesterday or why I've just walked into the room I'm in."

Catya laughed. "Well, that ain't too bad. There are plenty of older folks out there who can't even recall their own names."

"I guess there is that to it. Now, about me and my gun."

"Well...I had these calls from the Bundy creep."

"I thought you didn't talk with him no more."

"Like I said, *he* called *me*."

"Okay. And when he did, I hope you told him how happy you would be if he fell into an incinerator."

"Sure I did. But he had one interesting idea."

"Tell me."

Before outlining Bundy's interesting idea, Catya recounted its precursor, the tale of Brit PM Bruno Junkett having had half his bottom deflated by Norman Gubbins' toilet dart, thus rendering him half-assed.

Liking the idea, Uncle Silas chortled. "And the media were all over the story?" he said when the chortling was over.

"Yeah, only somehow it got sidelined by a tweet saying the whole thing was a Ripyurpanzov hit job."

"Holy hooley. Spooky business, huh?"

"Very."

"And let me guess...it was Bundy's interesting idea that got you thinking I could be the one to shoot off half of Klank's ass with my old Winchester."

"You're a good guesser, Uncle Silas. You keep the poachers away with it, right?"

"Sure I do, only I don't shoot them. Warning shots over their heads is all, mainly. I never injured a person, not ever. It goes against my beliefs."

"Even for *Klank*?"

"Even him. I know what the holy book says about eyes for eyes and teeth for teeth, but that always seemed to me a recipe for morons. If you hit them back after they've hit you, all you're doing is falling into their trap and playing the same lowdown game. How many times has that been an excuse for wars? Sure, Klank's a dumb, pompous, arrogant son of a bitch, but all shooting half his ass off would do would be to double his redneck and hillbilly fan base. He'd wear half an ass like a badge of honour and call out the National Guard to hunt down and kill the perp. Sorry for the spiel, but that's how I feel. Man, that even rhymes. Maybe there's a song further down the road."

Catya nodded and smiled. She'd half expected this response.

"No need for an apology, Uncle Silas."

"Plus, how'd I *get* to shoot him? Never heard of him visiting Mississippi creeks and I sure as hell ain't leaving mine to head off to Washington Dirty Closet where I'd never get close to him anyway."

"Yeah, that's true, too. Guess I wasn't thinking straight. But Uncle Silas?"

"Yeah?"

"Off the top of your head, do you have any other ideas how we could rain on his parade?"

"Sure I do. What the guy needs is a seminal dose of humiliation. What does he care about most?"

"Himself, money, being adored."

"Right. About the money there ain't nothing nobody can do, even the Revenue, hard though they try. And the money goes a long way to financing the adoration, so that leaves what, his hair maybe? Guy looks like he couldn't live without his hair."

A moment's silence while Catya thought this through before clapping her hands in glee. "You're *right*, that's the very thing. He's so damn proud of his hair he spends thousands of dollars a month on it. He loses that, he loses everything. Bald would drive him crazy."

"That's what I figure. Do we know anybody who could *make* him bald? Hard trick to pull, no?"

"Sure, but now you've put the idea in my head, I have a friend who may be able to help out."

"Tell me her name ain't Delilah."

Catya laughed. "Not even close."

"But even if he had no hair, he could get himself a wig," Uncle Silas continued. "One of them toopees."

"Not if we found a way to cut off all toupee suppliers to the White House."

"And how would we do that?"

"Put them out of business."

"By?"

"Ever heard of the way Covid-19 particles stored in false hair can eat through a person's scalp, then into the brain causing him or her to die much more horribly than ever previously imagined?"

"No."

"Me neither, but with so many social media bug theories on offer around the world, it wouldn't be too hard to add in this one. Tweetie, tweetie, tweet."

"So either he keeps his bald head and goes crazy, or he gets himself bug blasted and loses once and for all whatever is left of his mind? Nice choice."

"What I figure. Listen, thanks for giving me your time as always, Uncle Silas. It helped a lot. And thanks for pushing me at the hair idea."

"My pleasure, sweetheart. Keep me in the loop, okay?"

"I surely will. Now get down to writing that song with the 'spiel/feel' rhyme. Next time we talk I'd like to hear it."

"You got it," said Silas.

"Raaf, raaf," said Rufus, who was tired of Master's yacking and wanted his dinner.

Eight

Sir Keith Staniford whiled away the time awaiting George Ballentine's promised delivery of Norman Gubbins to the secret Chelsea address, wondering how long it would be before Conservative Party elders ran out of patience with Bruno Junkett and the U-turns and patent failures of him and his mealy-mouthed, crony-littered cabinet. That and the intriguing matter of the PM's bottom, which was already attracting opprobrium from hard-line, unforgiving, fox-hunting supporters in the shires, some of whom were already beginning to employ the phrase "half-arsed," Ripyurpanzov attack or no Ripyurpanzov attack. Tories were, after all, notorious for ditching leaders they no longer considered up to the job, and they would now doubtless be taking note of recent polls suggesting Sir Keith's popularity was outstripping Junkett's by a significant margin. As a realist, Sir Keith wasn't one to count his chickens, though. There wouldn't be another general election for four years, and everyone knew even a week was a long time in politics, so no point in getting overexcited just yet. First things first, like urging contacts in the US to get the vote out at *their* election and flush Klank down the toilet where he belonged. And, speaking of toilets, try to find out from Gubbins what had *really* happened to Junkett's bottom. Meanwhile, there was football to think about, even though most of the current season was likely to be played out behind Covid-closed doors. Still, as a supporter of Leeds United since his undergraduate days in the city, there were still the delights of their splendid promotion to the premier league to contemplate. When all else failed, there was always football to focus the mind and, at best, to cheer the soul.

It was as Sir Keith was thinking these thoughts that the street level door buzzer sounded and, looking down through the window of his fourth-floor flatlet, on the pavement he saw his old Accies' super-scorer colleague George Ballentine poking at the entrance panel with the index finger of one hand while the other struggled to hold upright the sagging figure Sir Keith took to be Norman Gubbins.

"Let us hope George hasn't done the bloke *too* much harm," said the ex-Director of Public Prosecutions, not wishing to be publicly prosecuted himself. But, fingers crossed, he pressed the button that would open the door. At least there was an elevator in the building so George wouldn't have to manhandle Gubbins up four flights of stairs.

Still, it was going on ten minutes before the knock came at Sir Keith's door, which he hurriedly opened before equally hurriedly jumping back, as an exhausted George let go of Norman, who fell in a crumpled heap flat on his face in the hallway.

"Good God, he's not dead, is he?" Sir Keith remarked to George as he stepped over the fallen Gubbins and into the secret flatlet.

"Nah, just a few tummy issues," said George. "Listen, he's moaning, so he can't be dead." Which was true enough. Norman was moaning for England. "Nnnnnn, aaahh, mmmmm, grrrng," he went, curling into a foetal ball and rubbing at his stomach.

"Something he's eaten?" asked Sir Keith, at which George said "only this" holding up his right fist, swivelling it about, and calling it a naughty boy before outlining the in-his-view perfectly cogent reasons for its use on Gubbins' belly.

"Only so much a bloke can take about the need for castrating Covid-infected Black Lives Matter males," he said.

"That bad?" said Sir Keith.

"*That* bad," said a sweating George, who might well have booted Norman in the head had Sir Keith not restrained him. "Anyhow, he's all yours now. Anytime you want another ratbag chased down, just give me a call."

"Hopefully that will never again be necessary," said Sir Keith as George headed to the door. "And I am extremely grateful for all your efforts. Send me the bill ASAP. Meanwhile, could I not persuade you to stick around another ten minutes to catch your breath? Don't know if you like chilled Guinness, but I've a few in the fridge. According to the old advert, they're good for you."

"Nnnnn, aaaah, mmmm, *bas*tard," said Norman, rolling with difficulty onto his back.

"Okay, I'm persuaded," said George, as Sir Keith steered him away from the writhing ex-PM-Whisperer towards a red leather couch. "Wouldn't want to leave you all alone to deal with this Nazi."

~ * ~

At much the same time as this was happening in Chelsea, Bruno Junkett was being delivered to his latest left buttock investigation appointment at the secret underground clinic to which, disguised as a corpse, he was driven in a blacked-out hearse. Once wheeled inside through a back door, he was met by the carefully vetted team consisting of a specialist bottom surgeon and two nurses in charge of repairing his left buttock, all three of whom were becoming increasingly suspicious as to the cause of his injury, Junkett's explanation of a monster mosquito in the lavatorium having failed to persuade them. It was only towards the end of his last visit they had dug out Norman's suction dart and it was that to which they now turned their attention.

"It is to this little fellow I suspect we should attribute your discomfort in the backside, PM," said consultant surgeon Mister Rupert Splinsky, specialist in both colorectal and butt lift operations, waggling Norman's dart in front of his nose as Bruno lay on the bed.

"What is it?" said Bruno, still attired in his ghoulish corpse outfit. "And make it quick, will you? Got the wretched Covid to deal with, dontcha know. Had it meself, as you might have heard, and it damn near killed me."

"Indeed," said Rupert, who had of course heard about Junkett's brush with Monsieur Coronavirus and continued to wonder if it were Long Covid that accounted for the acceleration in the PM's already disastrously erratic behaviour.

"I'm brim full of antibodies now, though, so I shouldn't get it again," Bruno boasted.

"So you keep saying in your interviews, PM," said Rupert, in whose scientific opinion Junkett might have dodged the bug altogether if he hadn't gone around believing it was no more than some super flu, shaking hands with anybody he met, and encouraging a then ingenuous nation to follow his example. Hence the swiftly increasing infection rate amongst not only UK citizens, but also a number of his colleagues. Furthermore, he was too fat, which couldn't have helped.

"Pretty tough type I am," said Bruno, who was always at his best when inventing lies about himself.

"So your press secretary keeps telling us, PM," growled Rupert. "Now would you like to hear about *this* little fellow, or wouldn't you?" he added, waggling Norman's dart some more.

"Ah *that*. What is it? But make it quick, I've got the bally Covid to deal with and…"

Splinksy knuckle-tapped at his forehead before practically shouting, "Some sort of suction dart that can enter the body and then suck out bits of it. In your case, the constituents of your left buttock, thereby leaving it empty, flaccid, and flat."

"Bally good job it didn't get into my head then, might have sucked my brains out," said Bruno, in what he thought of as a joke, although Rupert didn't even chuckle. After all, this was the PM who, if he had taken Covid seriously early enough, would have saved tens of thousands of lives, including those of Rupert's elderly uncle and two of his dedicated front-line A&E colleagues.

"And don't tell me it's got Ruskie written all over it," Bruno continued. "Some fake news story *that* was."

"Very probably, PM. But one wonders quite what sort of an automatic device it was that shot you in the bottom while you were defecating. Also, who planted it. I shall be passing the evidence along to Scotland Yard and MI6 to see if they have any records of such an event."

"No you won't, old boy. Not with my blessing. Let us just say it was some sort of freak incident, shall we? Meanwhile, if you could just stitch up the old botty, then pump it up the way you're being paid for, I won't withhold your pay cheque. Jolly inconvenient falling off chairs all the time. Does *nothing* for one's reputation. One has even heard the phrase 'half-arsed' muttered in the corridors of Parliament, which one does not find at *all* amusing."

"As the PM wishes," said Rupert, who was prepared to follow Bruno's advice where surgical matters were concerned, but reserved the right to follow up the dart's provenance with whomsoever he pleased. Having a sister who worked in the media industry, he might even pass on the whispered "half-arsed" witticism/accurate attribution. Strange it hadn't hit the headlines before, but maybe that had been due to the *faux* Ripyurpanzov narrative.

"Now," Rupert continued, waving in for assistance nurses Angelica Garcia and Florence Delacroix, "if the PM would care to take his pants down and roll onto to his, I'm afraid to say dangerously flabby belly, we'll get down to business."

"Oh, for Gawd's sake," protested Bruno.

But Angelica and Florence, both likely to become stateless or repatriated in a few months when Brexit kicked in, were in no mood to mollify the feelings of the guy they saw as their nemesis. It was therefore with little care that they ripped the PM's pants off, and with even less care, picked him up, turned him over, and dumped him on his stomach.

"Ouch, bloody *hell*," said Bruno, but his protestations were no longer of avail once the morpheme kicked in, he lost consciousness, and Rupert Splinsky went to work on his bottom, albeit with little intention of stitching up anything but an intermittent solution to the affliction. And a few little additives of his own invention.

By the time he was delivered back to Downing Street, Junkett might just as well have been the corpse he'd been disguised as on arrival at the hospital. No wonder, when he finally awoke needing advice on how to deal with the beast Staniford at PM's questions the next day, he screamed out the name Norman but, as we know, to no avail.

~ * ~

Having offered the Norman in question a chilled Guinness to make him feel better and told him to make himself at home on the red leather couch, Sir Keith Staniford took George Ballentine to the kitchenette for their chilled Guinness and a brief report of events leading to Gubbins' arrival at the secret Chelsea address.

"I'm sorry. It must've been pretty taxing for you," he said, when George had completed his résumé, which included not only Gubbins' desire to emasculate BLM males, but also a rough outline of his vision for a future Britain.

"What the bugger wants, best I can tell," said George, "is to kick out all foreigners, let no new ones in, castrate males of colour, Covid or no Covid, abolish Parliament, and have a dictator like Junkett and his cronies run the country instead."

Sir Keith smiled. He couldn't have put it better himself. Okay, in other circles he might have employed words like xenophobia, white male supremacy, oligarchy, and autocracy, but super-striker George had it just about spot on with regular language.

"So this is Gubbins' idea of the new normal, eh?" he said. "As if Boris and the bug hadn't already contributed enough to that, with the highest death rate in Europe, mass unemployment, twenty-three percent of people in poverty, hospitals overflowing and underequipped with PPE, and schools opening and closing on the latest government whim. And who benefits from all this? Who gets Covid-related contracts without external scrutiny? Gubbins' and Junkett's cronies, the sacrosanct Tory rich, that's who, just another case of *faux* pandering to the poor for their votes, while continuing to line the pockets of the least deserving. It's the usual populist doublespeak, when truths become indistinguishable from lies. The whole thing puts me in mind of an updated version of *1984* and Big Brother."

"Who?" said George, who wasn't much into literature.

Sir Keith gave him a quick rundown of Orwell's story and said he'd lend him the book one day.

"Meanwhile, I'd better get back to our guest. You sticking around?"

"Nah, I'll be on my way. There's a kick around with the lads in the park later and I don't want to miss it. Also, our boy might be a bit less chatty with me in the room."

"Okay, stay safe and see you soon," said Sir Keith, steering George past Norman, who scowled at him.

"See what I mean?" said George, heading for the door.

And so it was that the leader of Her Majesty's Opposition was left alone with one of the people on Earth he least liked. Diplomacy surely had to be the name of *this* game.

"So, Mister Gubbins, enjoy your Guinness, did you?" he kicked off with.

But Norman ignored the pleasantry and instead embarked on a lengthy diatribe in which he accused Sir Keith of kidnapping a high-ranking government official for which the punishment could amount to several years in the pokey without the option of early release for good behaviour.

This Sir Keith countered with the sort of insistent but restrained animus he had nurtured for years as a barrister and now displayed every Wednesday at Prime Minister's Questions with persistent demands for a clear road map in the government's handling of the pandemic, thereby reducing Bruno Junkett to hair-tugging and *ad hominem* counter accusations of tedious repetitiveness.

"You were *not* kidnapped, Mister Gubbins," he said. "You were invited perfectly politely to meet me for a private discussion. That your baser instincts concerning Black people like my friend George Ballentine should have led you to false conclusions is *your* problem, not mine."

That was when Norman threw his still half-full bottle of chilled Guinness at Sir Keith, who caught it at chest level, smiled, and carefully placed it on a coffee table.

"Now, now, Mister Gubbins, let us not get over-excited, shall we?"

Which, of course, excited Norman a whole lot more.

"Fucking *Soci*alist," he spluttered. "Probably being paid off by the Kremlin."

Sir Keith gave a gentle smile. "This despite the incontrovertible evidence of Ripyurpanzov's Internet meddling in not only the Brexit fiasco but also Klank's and *your* boss's election to the top jobs. Ever wondered why that might have been, Mister Gubbins? Or did you and poor old Bruno just turn a happily blind eye to such felicitous support from a well-practised dictator seeking pals across the globe? And *I'm* the one you're accusing of being Russia's puppet?"

It wasn't wise of Norman to spring from the red leather couch at this moment and ball a fist because, like George some hours earlier, Sir Keith merely caught it, squeezed somewhat less gently than George and told Norman to sit back down and face reality.

"Do you and your master Junkett *really* believe you have reason other than the gratification of your personal desires for stealing the painfully won right over centuries for male and female individuals, including Black ones, to determine whom they trust to represent and govern them through a democratically elected parliament?"

"Well answer me, man," Sir Keith continued as Norman stared at the ceiling as if it might have the answer. "And when you've reached your conclusion, I'd be interested to know what insider information you might have about the fate of Bruno's bottom."

Nine

At the desk in the Oval Office he'd had transformed into a Square Office replete with a miniature putting green and photos of himself signing presidential decrees, Dougal Klank was at his truth-distorting happiest firing off tweets in all directions at supposed and real enemies. His rival in the upcoming election, Jack Bailey, for example, was a covert homosexual with a predilection for underage Black boys, a FACT he was trying to cover up by putting an ass-kissing Black woman on his ticket as running mate. Oh, and incidentally, said Black woman wasn't even a proper American, because she'd been born of mixed parentage in Bongo-Bongo-land. *Plus,* Bailey was a cowardly Vietnam War draft dodger, which was a pity, because if he'd fought, he might have joined the "suckers" and "losers" who'd been dumb enough to get killed over there. No mention of Klank's Vietnam excuse, of course, namely being too busy back then dodging sexually transmitted diseases.

With this little barrage off his chest, he turned his attention to psephological issues, namely those that could most easily be distorted to ensure his election victory. Prime amongst those was the suggestion that, given the notorious unreliability of the US Postal

Service, it would be wise for voters in swing states, particularly those with a decent Klank base, to vote twice, once in the proper manner and another time—just in case the post was still working—by mail. It was all very reminiscent of the old Irish advice to voters: vote early and vote often. That nobody with any acumen in the field might have noticed this counsel amounted to election rigging did not cross Klank's sick mind. Why? Because if you're a dyed-in-the-blood misogynistic, xenophobic, mendacious, narcissistic sociopath—like his pal Junkett over in the UK—such niceties simply do not occur. Which was also why Klank figured that, even if he lost the election, he would declare the result null and void and refuse to leave office, thereby triggering the sort of constitutional crisis he would relish and blame on everybody but himself. And if he won, he would have his detractors thrown in jail accused of worshipping FAKE!! gods, and continue to be the most talked about and photographed person on the world's stage. Had he heard of Oscar Wilde, he might have recognised the dramatist and poet's declaration that "there is only one thing in the world worse than being talked about, and that is not being talked about," but Klank hadn't heard of Oscar Wilde, and thus considered the trademark solely his. Such was the acumen the ex-host of *Apprentice* brought to the White House and why he so relished being headline news, even if it was bad. That, and the right to hire sycophants on the least excuse and fire them the moment he sensed even a whiff of criticism. *Vide* Sam Bundy, for example. No wonder Bruno Junkett had been so impressed by the president's verbiage when visiting Washington during his brief and ignominious spell as UK Foreign Secretary.

*Any*way, it was as Klank was taking a brief respite from lying, and wandered over to a wall mirror to check on his hair, the intercom message from Hank O'Henry came through that his new coiffeuse was in an ante-chamber ready for a spot of primping, tweaking, and perfecting. Only Klank remembered the previous one.

"Check out the creds before you let her anywhere near me," he barked. "The last bitch fucking near set my hair on fire."

Not "me" on fire, please note, "my hair."

There was an hiatus while a new and improved Maggie McKenzie, now operating as Annie L'Amour, was checked against stored images of Margot Komova and came out clear as a whistle. But then Maggie was good at makeovers; it was her business, after all. Now she had jet-black hair at waist level, a post-facial suggesting a provenance somewhere along the Côte d'Azur and, after practice sessions with New York-based French phonetician called Docteur François Dubois, the sexiest Anglo-French accent since Brigitte Bardot's way back in the twentieth century. Then there was the couture to take into account, which might be best described as expensively tasteless and scanty, emphasizing as it did her cleavage in a frilly red blouse open practically to the navel and white jeans so tight around the backside they would have split if she had sat down.

"This ain't the last bitch, boss," came the intercom message from Hank when the hiatus was over. "This is a whole new dame and I think you're gonna like her."

"Ookay, so send her in. She has a Covid-negative certificate, right? Nobody comes near me with the bug, you know that, Hank."

"Also checked, boss."

"Good. Got my rep to think of when it comes to the bug."

"Yes *sir*, she's clean," said Hank, well aware of how much the president hyped his role as world saviour with the new (un-trialled) vaccine he'd paid a previously unheard-of lab in one of his companies to develop, while turning a blind eye and deaf ear to the daily exponential rises in Covid cases and deaths across the country, saying they were yet more "fake news" and "we are in a good place." Klank certainly would be if the vaccine ever got distributed and the dollars started rolling in.

Once he was convinced she was bug free, Maggie McKenzie was ushered into the presidential presence a second occasion, and this time, albeit through gritted teeth, submitted herself to Klank's saddo playbook of ass grabbing and breast tweaking. After all, if Catya's and her Uncle Silas's idea of hair cropping with her assistance were to reach fruition, the next time she came here, she would need to be a *persona* very *grata* indeed. The performance was humiliating but, as Maggie saw it, all in a good cause. And mercifully this time, Klank didn't try to get his dick out.

And the hour-long session—including compliments such as "Boy, this is the most beautiful hair I've ever seen," and "Geez, look how it shines"—went well as Klank preened in front of the mirror while Maggie treated his locks to top-of-the-range sprays and gels. When she was shepherded out of the Square Office by Hank, she was heartened to hear Klank call after her, "Come again anytime you want, babe. You're my kinda gal."

"Bet on it, honeychile," she called back in a peculiar Creole franglais.

"To give you the haircut of your life," she whispered very *sotto voce* and well out of earshot.

Not that Klank paid any attention. He was too busy tweeting about how Jack Bailey only had one testicle and even that was unreliable. "AFTER THE ELECTION THE GUY'LL HAVE NO BALLS AT ALL," he concluded triumphantly.

~ * ~

Rupert Splinsky's younger sister was named Ramona, but no longer Splinsky because on a whim she'd married the upcoming wannabe social media mogul, Henry Smith, who, reckoning such a moniker would get him nowhere in show business, had changed his name to Enrique Schmidt on the basis it would render him tantalizingly international and mysteriously romantic. That was why Ramona no longer went by Splinsky, a name she'd never much liked anyway, but Schmidt instead. Not that she any longer much liked that either, or indeed Enrique himself. Okay, it wasn't Henry's fault he'd been born in Yorkshire and sported no higher education quals. In fact, it was for precisely those reasons Ramona had fallen for him, a case of opposite poles attracting. Good looks, ambition, and his "call a spade a spade" philosophy were quite enough for Ramona in the early days of their romance. It was Enrique's metamorphosis into Northern-boy-made-good London pseud she'd found hard to swallow. Fine, so he now owned and operated an AI-driven online "news and views" platform called JawJaw, having ditched his first foray into "old-fashioned" print journalism *The Daily Grouse*, on the grounds nobody read paper any more. But this wasn't the nitty gritty Henry Smith she had first fallen for. This was a whole new person whose working class origins now poo-pooed her Oxford first class PPE degree as "footling" by comparison with his market prowess. And Ramona couldn't deny the money was coming in—*how* she didn't know—and the basement flat he'd bought outright in Hampstead was better by a country mile than anything she could ever have afforded as an occasional contributor to the few liberally minded national newspapers prepared to give her the occasional column inch. In these circumstances, brother Rupert's call about Bruno's bottom came as the potential blockbuster that might just help her pay her way, balance up the marriage respect books, *and* prove the market value of a degree in philosophy, politics and economics.

Obviously, Rupert had thought carefully before delivering such a confidentiality breaking and thus potentially career-ending message, in the knowledge Junkett would almost certainly deduce its origin and raise hell but, Rupert reflected, let him. There were times in a person's life when they had to stand up for the ethics in which they believed and let the devil take the hindmost. And Rupert believed Junkett to be a lying confidence trickster who apparently believed that what he claimed to be a world-beating set of anti-Covid policies would assure his rise to national sainthood at the same time as running an economy open to everyone, thereby keeping both options on the table. A shame from Junkett's point of view this mismatched balance of health and wealth wasn't working, but did Junkett care? The hell he did, despite the shrieks of alarm from the NHS as hospital Covid admissions rose to record levels. On and on he blustered with blithe optimism and successive U-turns on all fronts, which, as a strict adherent to the Hippocratic code, was in Rupert's view a criminally inverted logic deserving of national disgrace. After all, a healthy economy—which the UK's currently was *not*—was unlikely to be generated by a population decimated and demoralised by the bug, whereas it might just survive and prosper if the priority were that folk should live and fight another day. Okay, Bruno's government was borrowing billions beyond the nation's means to support the sorts of industries it fancied with furlough schemes, but that was just unsustainable window dressing. And if Mister Rupert Splinsky became the scapegoat along the path to the recognition of these conclusions, well so be it. Should the story about the PM's bottom as far as Rupert knew it—he didn't, of course, know of Gubbins' involvement—and its "half-arsed" tag go viral and Rupert be dragged through the courts, he would at the very least be telling the truth, which was a precious commodity in the current atmosphere of knowingly mendacious "alternative news." If a person liked swimming, he reckoned, it should always be in deep water and against the tide.

"You're kidding me, Rupe," said Ramona when she'd stopped laughing.

"I kid you not, sis. He was somehow shot in the bottom while taking a number two."

"So the Ripyurpanzov story was just a cover-up."

"One can only assume so."

"But nobody can hide in a lavatory bowl," said Ramona logically enough. "Not even a teeny-weeny tiny person. Unless we're talking elves or something."

"Which we obviously are not."

"Then what?"

"My best guess would be a super accelerated water flushing system in which the dart was hidden and primed for use when activated remotely."

"Dart?"

"We dug it out of his left bum cheek on the last visit. It's a clever little chap, able to suck body mass from whatever it hits."

"And it's not Russian?"

"We don't think so, but there's no stamp on it saying 'Made in the UK,' either."

"Blimey. And you've no idea who might have engineered this caper?"

"None, although..."

"Hit me," said Ramona.

"A political opponent is a possibility. While under the knife, Junkett complained bitterly about chuckled whispers of his "half-arsedness" in the corridors of power, by which I assumed he meant Parliament.""

In Ramona's super-brain, so many little lights went on so instantaneously it was hard to separate one from the other, but after only a few moments of analytical reflection, she had the story she just knew Enrique would kill for, the one implicating in the dastardly crime either some renegade Tory overlooked for promotion or—better still—the Leader of the Opposition, Sir Keith Staniford. Viral was the sort of response she would be expecting from such a post, particularly given the extra spice of lavatorial humour and the titillating inclusion of "half-arsed" when applied both literally and metaphorically. No doubt what remained of the radical print and broadcast media would pounce on such a story, in exchange for which Enrique could screw them for a few hundred thousand quid. And that was before the giant leap forward against its social media rivals JawJaw would take.

"Wow, thanks so much, Rupe. You're a star," she said.

"I wouldn't go that far, sis. Just one thing, though."

"Name it."

"I'd be grateful for no attribution of the source of your story. No doubt Junkett'll pin it on me in due course, but I'd prefer that to be later rather than sooner."

"You've got it, Rupe. No way would Enrique or I go naming names."

"Good, great. Meanwhile, you and he stay safe. The damn bug is back big time, as I'm sure you're aware."

"Tell me about it."

"And government 'policy' relies solely on them licking their fingers, sticking them in the air, and seeing which way the wind's blowing."

"True enough. You know what I'd like best from the story you've given us?"

"I can guess, but tell me anyway."

"Two things. Number one, some clever pants graffiti artist sneaks past Downing Street police patrols at the dead of night and paints 'Half-Arsed' all over number ten's door."

Rupert chuckled. "Ever since you were a little kid, you always lived somewhere off in fantasy land. Am I right?"

"You are, Rupe. But…"

"But what?"

"'If you don't have a dream, how you gonna have a dream come true?'" Ramona quoted from *South Pacific*.

"And your other fantasy?"

"Is more realistic. Just *think* how wonderful it would be to see Trafalgar Square jammed with protesters wearing toilet bowl-shaped hats and waving banners reading QUIT NOW HALF-ARSED BRUNO!!! We could become QNHAB just like Black Lives Matter became BLM."

"That could be fun indeed," said Rupert, who had never been a fan of the clown now in Number Ten, and would happily have sliced off his *right* buttock with an 'accidental' slip of his scalpel. A case of "Ooops, PM, there goes the other one."

"*Any*how," he continued, "enough for now. I've got other bottoms to attend to. Good luck with the info."

"Thanks. And thanks *for* it. I'll keep you posted," said Ramona cutting the call.

Ten

"So, Mister Gubbins, to the question of Bruno Junkett's bottom," said Sir Keith Staniford, at which Norman writhed and took an unnatural interest in a pot plant.

"Mister Gubbins?" Sir Keith continued, intuiting insider knowledge/guilt from more courtroom appearances than he could remember as a Queen's Counsel. Mind you, a person didn't need to be a QC to interpret the body language. What did help, however, was the professional approach to determining its source.

"Might it be fair to assume that you, as the PM's most trusted advisor, have some insight into how the injury was sustained? Always assuming the Russian angle was a hoax, that is," was his first question.

"PM's *only* adviser," Norman corrected, blinking up from the pot plant fascination.

Which was a good start for Sir Keith. Hubris was always an exploitable means of loosening the tongue.

"My apologies. *Only* adviser. Which would lead one to assume you are intimate with his daily routine."

"I didn't go to the bloody toilet with him, if that's what you're getting at," Norman growled.

"Toilet?" said Sir Keith, also spotting the "didn't."

"Manner of speaking," said Norman, knitting his fingers over the unforced toilet error. "I wasn't his nanny," he added.

"I see. And may one ask why you are using the past tense in relation to your service at Downing Street?"

Which was when Norman again sprang up from the red leather couch and *again* balled his fist, which for the second time Sir Keith caught and squeezed before returning Norman to the couch screaming, "You can't keep me here under duress. I'm not a prisoner in the dock being asked incriminating questions."

"Quite so, Mister Gubbins. As I said at the outset, you are an invited guest, but as such I would be obliged if you would behave like one, as opposed to throwing bottles about and attempting to hit me. I am, however, a curious man and would be obliged if you would answer my questions. Thereafter, you shall be free to leave."

"Trotskyite bastard," said Norman. But he sat back down.

"That's better, Mister Gubbins. *Now*, is one to assume from the past tense you are no longer in Junkett's employ? One wonders, for example, what you were doing in Penzance whither my colleague Mister Ballentine traced you in your Winnebago. One had thought during a pandemic that all but essential travel had been banned, especially for top-ranking types like you, although there was that other unauthorised and unexplained little trip up north you took, wasn't there? Fairly hit the headlines, that did. But again on the Cornwall trip you must have broken the rules, or law, or advice, or whatever it is Bruno calls his midnight brainwaves."

Norman took to breathing irregularly. "Huh-*how* did you know about...?" he managed to splutter.

"Penzance? As I told you, from my colleague Mister Ballentine, who operates a far more efficient tracking facility than the world-beatingly laughable eighteen million pounds worth of Covid testing and tracing equipment blazoned by your PM on your advice. Now perhaps we might return to *my* questions, specifically the one relating to Bruno's bottom. Albeit as only a slip of the tongue you mentioned toilet visits, although you also employed the past tense in regard to your position at Downing Street. I would, of course, be interested in whether or not you are still in post there."

Norman hung his head, breathed even less regularly, and mewled.

"Mister Gubbins?" said Sir Keith, fearful he might have sparked some underlying health condition. After all, causing a government adviser a stroke or worse wouldn't look at all good in the media and would likely reverse his current fragile lead in the popularity polls.

Norman chuckled inwardly while clutching his throat and choking. It was a routine he'd used to his advantage during many awkward moments in his past, dating all the way back to school.

"Mister *Gubbins*," said a now alarmed Sir Keith. "Something the matter?"

Norman jabbed at the area on his chest beneath which lay the heart, blinked twenty-five times, that being the optimal blink number in his experience, and gurgled, "Nuh-need muh-my puh-pills."

"Got them with you? In your pocket perhaps," said Sir Keith, hastening to the red leather couch over which Norman was slumped sideways.

Norman shook his head six times—also an optimal number—and whispered, "Uh-at huh-home. Guh-get me a tuh-taxi."

Which Sir Keith did straightway, keen to avoid headlines in the next day's feral alt-right press like, "Gubbins Dead After Staniford Third Degree."

While he watched on from his third-floor window, it wasn't until Norman was safely in the cab, leaning out of the window, sticking out his tongue, and flipping his third finger in the air that Sir Keith realized what a fool he'd been played for. Nonetheless, the conversation served to underline the suspicion Gubbins had indeed something to hide in Junkett's bottom issue, which would also explain his use of the past tense when referring to his time in Downing Street.

"Mmm, curiouser and curiouser," mused Sir Keith.

~ * ~

Prior to coiffeuse Maggie McKenzie/Annie L'Amour's entry to Klank's Square Office for his penultimate hairdo she, Catya Rampersad, *and* Hank O'Henry had come together for a top secret meeting to discuss strategy when the day came for Maggie to put into practice the hair cropping idea spawned by Catya's Uncle Silas. It was only after careful consideration the two women had decided to trust Hank and get him on board for the enterprise. After all, never mind his assurances of support to Maggie, who was to know if deep down he *was* what his White House position suggested: namely a Klank sycophant and protector who, if he learned of their intentions, would simply shop them to his boss, landing them both in deep doo-doo.

What had finally persuaded them, though, were the contents of the sealed envelope he had pressed into Maggie's hand as she left the White House. In them he had disclosed what he swore on all that was holy was his true role in the Klank zone, which was as a double agent. Not a Russian spy or anything dramatic of that sort, but merely an "ordinary guy getting close to the bastard" to expose and hopefully revenge the "inhumanity of a president who could have allowed so many hundreds of thousands of folk to die from Covid-19 by pretending it wasn't happening." This was what he termed "reporting back from the war zone." Which were the words that persuaded Catya of his credibility. Similar indeed they were to the way she had described her own job to Uncle Silas when she talked about reporting back from the front line. Maggie, too, was persuaded. The words she had appreciated were, "I'm so happy you set the fuck's hair on fire. You get any more plans to hurt him, tell me about them. My number is enclosed."

In preparation for the Annie L'Amour visit, therefore, Catya and Maggie had made sure to contact Hank and give him the lowdown on their new scheme. Who better to ensure Annie had left the premises safely before heading off with Catya down to her hideaway up Uncle Silas's Mississippi creek? All face-masked, they met outside the same Starbucks on Pennsylvania Ave where Catya and Maggie had fallen in love with each other—although they *still* didn't know it.

After the how're-you-doings and so on, it was Catya who got the trio down to business by first off explaining their plan to Hank, who shook his head in admiration.

"That sure is the neatest idea," he said. "There is nothing the asshole treasures more than his hair, otherwise he wouldn't have spent seventy thousand dollars getting it fixed in recent days. But tell me, how're you going to cut it off without him knowing? He'll fight you for it, you can be damn sure."

"Not if he's asleep," said Catya, raising her eyebrows and thumbing the plunger of an imaginary syringe.

"You could *do* that?" Hank asked Maggie.

"Sure I could. Long time ago, I was a hospital hairdresser in NYC. All kindsa tricks a gal can learn on the wards if she keeps her eyes open. Where the best veins are, all that sort of shit. With Klank, though, I'm aiming straight for the ass."

Hank laughed. "I'd sure like to be a fly on *that* wall."

Catya sympathised. "Me, too, believe me. But you and I have different jobs, Hank...you as inside lookout guy and me as getaway driver. It's Annie L'Amour here who gets all the fun.

"Okay, deal. Anyhow, when he's off in la-la-land, it's goodbye hair, right?"

"Right," said Maggie.

"But won't it grow again?"

"Not for a *very* long time, or maybe never after the root-death tincture I can get from a pal of mine at the Misericordia hospital on East Eighty-Sixth Street. Then we put a nice little rubbery skullcap on top."

Hank nodded. "But even so, he could still get himself one of them toopees."

This was the same argument Uncle Silas had prosecuted, so Catya gave the same explanation about the sad reputation Covid-19-infected toupées had for eating through the skull, causing irreparable brain damage.

"Which is *true*?" said Hank.

"So long as folk are dumb enough to believe every little thing the Internet tells them, sure it is," said Catya.

Hank smiled. "I guess there is that to it. Man, wouldn't I just love to see his face the first time he looks in the mirror."

"Which is the honour reserved for you," said Maggie, "while I get the hell outta there in double quick time, jump in Catya's car, and head south to New Orleans."

"You gals are something else," said Hank, accepting the offer of a Pall Mall from Catya. "So let's make the date and I'll get every little thing in A-one order."

With that, Hank and Catya went back to their White House duties, while Maggie McKenzie hiked into the city to buy herself a syringe or two for a spot of thumb-strengthening practice.

~ * ~

It was a sultry, steamy, late evening when Silas Baudoin got the call from his niece Catya to say all was set for Klank's big haircut experience; it was just a matter of finding a good date. Sitting on his old rocker out on the porch of his cabin with Rufus sprawled across his feet, he'd been listening to the songs of reed warblers and corncrakes and suchlike, and accompanying them on his old Gibson to the tune of "Up A Lazy River." Okay, the noonday sun was long gone, but up his creek the waters were still lazy, and Silas liked it that way. What was the need for hurry? And it wasn't only homegrown classics that passed down the advice. Poor old John Beatle—shot down in his prime by an American—had it pretty much right, too, in "I'm Only Sleeping." Silas lay back and played the song in his head until the words he wanted came, the ones about folk finding out there was no need for them to run everywhere at silly speeds. No wonder the damn doctors and shrinks made such good livings with mental and physical breakdowns every which way you looked. And now there was the Corvid-19 to drive them either stir crazy or to their graves. One in every fifty Americans dead or dying, according to informed sources, while the criminal in the White House played golf like nothing was happening, never mind pretending the ice caps at the poles weren't melting. Talk about a world gone crazy. Silas was pretty glad he wouldn't be around too much longer to witness any more of this shit...it wasn't as though he'd be much missed, except by the family. But that was okay. Only fools looked back on their lives and thought they'd mattered. No melancholia for Silas Baudoin, therefore, no siree. It was while he was remembering another of John Beatle's songs, "Working Class Hero," and how there was room at the top but first you had to learn how to smile while you killed, that Catya came through with the news.

"And when we're done, would it be okay for me to bring my new best friend, Maggie, down home to stay with you a while?"

"She the cutter?"

"She's the cutter, Uncle Silas, and she's going to need to lay low for what may be a long while."

"So bring the national heroine to me. Nobody gonna find her here," said Silas. "She pretty?"

"As a picture. Blonde, beautiful, and her own person, if you follow."

"Sound just like my kinda gal."

Catya laughed. "There is a teeny weeny age difference between the two of you, Uncle Silas."

"Only an old man kidding you, babe. Chances are she'll pretty soon get bored around a geriatric like me. Also, hey, if you're bringing her down here, are you staying over, too?"

"Maybe for the day or two of leave I've got coming, but if I'm away from the Shite House too long, there would be questions. Also, I need to look out for the Hank guy I told you about, make sure nobody starts asking him difficult questions about how the crazy hair cutter got past his defences."

"Okey dokey, but let's make the best of the coupla days we do have. Have us a little celebration. Maybe get your folks around?"

"Sounds good to me. Meanwhile, look out for the news on your phone. One thing you can be sure of, though."

"Which is?"

"There won't be any pictures of Klank on it. He'll be banging his bald head against a wall someplace well away from any cameras. Unless maybe we can get Hank to record the event for history."

Silas was still laughing after Catya had wished him well, thanked him for hosting Maggie, and cut the call.

Eleven

Given the terms and conditions of his $5 million bail bond while he awaited trial, Sam Bundy had little option but to shelve any escapist travel plans and to self-isolate at his Harvard University special alumnus home, like someone who has just tested positive for Covid. Humiliating for a person of his global populist influence, of course it was, but better that than try to do a runner and get shot for his troubles or, worse still, to screw up the naming-of-names plea bargaining plans he dearly hoped would reduce his sentence from twenty years to zero. In addition, it gave him an unaccustomed space in which to think outside the box he had created for himself over so many years, the one in which he featured as a covert super-brain puppet master, jerking the strings of ungrateful morons like Dougal fucking Klank all the way to supreme power. What, Sam was beginning to wonder, would there be *outside* that box? He also remembered the brief conversation he'd had with Norman Gubbins, in which the guy told him about Junkett's bottom and then went off on a riff about great men being bad men and absolute power corrupting absolutely.

For a number of self-isolating days—six to be precise—such thoughts went around, around, and *around* Bundy's whiskey befuddled mind until they had pretty much become an obsession. And you know how it is with obsessions, how they won't leave you alone and keep waking you up in the middle of the night sweating so there is no chance of going back to sleep perchance to dream of anything other than the obsession.

It was at three forty-three a.m. on the seventh of such days that, kicking at his duvet and flailing his arms, Sam experienced what might be thought of as the epiphany that helped him recognise what lay outside the box he had locked himself into—namely nothing, except for the madness that went with nothingness.

"Aaaaaggghh, eeeek, gggrrrung, screeerch," he shrieked, sitting bolt upright against the headboard with such suddenness that one of his flailing arms whacked his chin and loosened several teeth, while the other knocked out the bedside light. In their sockets, his eyeballs took to revolving, and down his chin ran both spittle and blood from the newly wonky teeth.

And what was the cause of this sudden plunge into hysterical delirium? The truth, that was what. The horrible, diabolical realisation his whole life so far had been a sham devoted to what he had always believed to be the unerring, glittering successes emanating from his unquestioned brilliance, a belief that now lay in shreds. And not just because he'd been fired by Klank, or accused of crimes that could land him in jail for the better part of the rest of his life, worse still because he now recognised himself as one of T.S. Eliot's hollow stuffed men with eyes which could not be met in dreams—and the recognition was understandably terrifying. It was all very well for R.D. Laing to suggest insanity to be the rational adjustment to an insane world, but the political world Sam Bundy reckoned he'd ushered in had been in his view entirely *sane*, or at the very least profitable. Now, rather in the manner of Kafka's Gregor Samsa in *Metamorphosis*, he had awoken from "uneasy dreams" a "gigantic insect" and faced the horrors of the "unknown unknowns, the ones we don't know we don't know," as outlined in relation to the Iraq war by Donald Rumsfeld in 2002.

Bundy had taken at Harvard an in-his-view sensible MBA, but in the process of studying for it, he had inevitably come across the lit, psych and pol sci students who back then he'd dismissed as "arty farties," but whose references during boozy evenings now echoed around his fractured mind with an eerie, unworldly, and hideous resonance.

It was at four fifty-eight on that dramatic morning that Bundy stopped shrieking, mopped his damaged teeth, took a long hard swig from his bedside bottle of Jim Beam and took to mewling much in the manner of Norman Gubbins while engineering his escape from Sir Keith's Staniford's secret Chelsea flat, only without such a practical objective. These were non-programmatic, ingressive mewls, whose only purpose was to give vent to his mounting sense of self-pity, although they were punctured from time to time by blasts of vocal fury aimed at the ungrateful planet Earth.

So, for example, one minute Bundy would be mewling, "Poor me, *poor* me, why *me*?" and the next he would be hollering, "*FUCK YOU* and your *MOTHER* fuckwit world, I'm a-coming to getcha."

It was these words robotically repeated over and over, plus many others of the same ilk, and the hammering on the party wall with the broken Jim Beam bottle, which, at five twenty-three a.m., awakened Sam's next-door neighbour, ex-professor of Jungian psychiatry Maximilian Zhillikopf, who had trouble sleeping anyway and didn't need this racket.

"Whadda *hell*?" mumbled Max, fumbling under the pillow for his phone.

Which was how it came to pass that Max alerted the emergency services to a raving lunatic next door, who in his view might be suffering from an as yet undiagnosed, possibly asymptomatic, neural version of Covid-19. Which was why, by seven thirteen, a still writhing and mewling Sam Bundy found himself strapped to a gurney and heading towards a wah-wah-wahing, blue-lights-flashing ambulance.

Which is where we shall leave him for the moment. Just let's say this wasn't the best day—or indeed year—in Sam Bundy's life so far.

~ * ~

Ramona Smith/Schmidt was right when she surmised husband Henry/Enrique would like the "half-arsed PM" lavatory story. He didn't just like it, he *lurved* it. The minute she passed on the info, pound and dollar signs took to flashing before his eyes and he gave her a smackeroo on the lips for her troubles.

"Some sleuth you must be, Ramo," he said, when the smackeroo was over. "Where d'you get it? You sure it's one hundred percent kosher?"

Not that very many of the stories Enrique unleashed on JawJaw were anything like kosher, the majority being the mindless blethering of bloggers with nothing better to do than court what they considered "fame" by posting, for example, life-threatening cures for Covid, such as eating horse manure or suggesting the illness was being spread by Martians with plans for earth domination. Which, given there was no human editorial board, only an algorithm controlling the platform, meant pretty soon they had followers swearing blind that chewing mouse testicles ensured not only Covid survival but also improved sexual performance. When first launched, JawJaw had truly been a means for folk using technology to "come together," as John Lennon had it, but these days it was the technology using *them* as fodder. All of which was making Enrique Schmidt money beyond even his imagining. Nonetheless, when it came to Ramona's "half-arsed PM" story, even Enrique wanted reassurance. The last thing he needed was some *tight*-arsed parliamentary committee shutting down JawJaw for false allegations as to the nature of Bruno's *half*-arsedness.

Ramona was pleased at the smackeroo, but also keen to press home her advantage and thereby go some way to redressing both the financial and intellectual balances in their relationship. Which was why she said, "Not bad for a person with only a 'footling' PPE from Oxford, eh?"

Which blindsided Enrique in the midst of his euphoria.

"Pardon?" he said.

"You know what I'm talking about, Henry."

Which discombobulated Enrique even further, particularly given the way he'd recently insisted on no longer *ever* being called Henry and even Enrique had been reduced to the sexier diminutive "Rickie."

"As a matter of fact, no, I really don't," said Rickie/Enrique/Henry.

"It's the way you used to downgrade my intelligence and put me in what you thought of as my wifely place," Ramona explained. "But if you want evidence of the authenticity of the PM's "half-arsed" story, you will now apologize for previous, what shall I say 'misunderstandings,' and agree to a little more respect and a fifty-fifty split in all earnings accrued to JawJaw should the story go viral."

"Wow," said Rickie/Enrique/Henry, now back in the familiar territory of profit margin haggling, albeit for the first time with his wife.

"Take it or leave it," said Ramona. "Take it and we'll be able to flog the story for all its worth. Leave it, and I'm out of here to sell to the highest bidder. Of whom I'm sure there will be many."

This being the first time Ramona had raised her head above the parapet in the three years of their marriage, Rickie/Enrique/Henry was dumbfounded and, deserted by language, went for the tried and tested bottom-stroking routine which normally had Ramona giggling her way out of some minor tiff or other. Not this time, though.

"Hands off," said Ramona, swatting at the groping fingers and leaving Rickie/Enrique/Henry yet further perplexed. Normally it would have been knickers off and sex on the carpet after such a move, but this was apparently the even *newer* normal.

"Um, erm...um," said Rickie/Enrique/Henry, lacking the sorts of emotional vocabulary needed to cope with such a situation. Proper Yorkshire menfolk didn't have emotional vocabularies, considering them only fit for womenfolk or nancy boys.

"Well, is it a 'take' or is it a 'leave'?" asked Ramona, going for the jugular.

"Um, erm...um," repeated her husband, flapping his swatted hand about and wincing.

At which Ramona made the age-old female mistake of feeling a quasi-maternal pity for the male she'd humbled, and the need to compensate.

"Sorry about the hand," she said. "Don't know my own strength."

"No problemo, I'm sure it'll be fine," said Rickie/Enrique/Henry manfully.

"Look, we need to talk, Rickie," said Ramona. "I'll fetch us a bottle of Plonque Française from the fridge, okay?"

"Okay."

"Then we'll sit together and have a little chat."

"Okay," said Rickie/Enrique/Henry, heading for the top-of-the-range Harrods Sofology sofa and flopping down on it.

The "little chat"—too tedious to report in detail here—lasted seventy-six minutes, during which Ramona spoke for seventy-one and Rickie's occasional responses amounted to a total of five. Not for nothing had Ramona won plaudits for her contributions to Oxford Union debates.

*Any*way, cutting to the as it turned out to be marriage-saving conclusion to the discussion, Rickie caved in to the fifty-fifty split and—after the opening of a second bottle of Plonque Française—even offered to raise the stakes to sixty-forty in Ramona's favour. Which in all fairness she refused. The crucial part of this conversation, however, was Rickie/Enrique/Henry forgetting his original question concerning Ramona's source for the Bruno's bottom story and Ramona therefore never having to disclose brother Rupert's part in it.

So it was that the lavatorial tale of Junkett's half-arsedness was loosed upon social media outlets and billions of folk worldwide up to the gunnels in coronavirus lockdowns and sorely in need of something to laugh at. Translations both literal and metaphorical of "half-arsed" were needed, of course, but polyglot Ramona took care of all that.

Twelve

After the narrow squeak with Sir Keith Staniford, Norman Gubbins instructed his face-masked Black cab driver Kelvin Grimes to take him to Kentish Town and not to spare the horses, an order Kelvin refused unless Norman also masked up.

"No mask no ride," said Kelvin, an emigré Liverpudlian who didn't like toffs at the best of times and wasn't ready to catch the virus from one at the worst of times. Also, he'd seen this geezer's picture in the papers. Some PM's adviser he was, and Kelvin liked Tory toffs even less than he liked ordinary ones.

"Now look you here, my man," Norman protested, but to no avail.

"Don't you 'my man' me, pal. Put your mask on or get out of my cab. You know the rules."

Which, having composed most of them while Bruno Junkett scribbled notes, Norman obviously did. Only these were rules for the little people, not for Norman Gubbins, who replied, "Haven't got one, don't need one. Been tested and I'm negative."

"Yeah, sure, and I'm Peter Pan. Show me the certificate. Test and trace system in this country's up its arse, anyway, whatever the knobhead PM and his sicko cronies say. World-beating right? Well, you can tell that to the Marines. Mobile phones with an app that tells you you've just walked past an infected person? Bollocks. Don't s'pose you've heard of how a person can catch Covid twice either, have you?" said Kelvin, whose judgement of the pandemic, its treatment and potential outcomes, depended solely on advice from WHO scientists. In his view, nobody in his or her right mind would listen to advice from glossy-faced, receding-hairline boys masquerading as government ministers, crippled in their daily "progress reports" by the Janus-facedly pretence it was the health of the potential Covid sufferer in lockdown they cared for more than the wealth of their Tory grandees. Then there was their shaggy-haired lying buffoon of a boss, who not even a street beggar would trust not to steal his last sandwich. No, no, when it came to facts, it was the experts Kelvin listened to.

"Well, *have* you?" he repeated.

Sensing opprobrium to which he was not accustomed, Norman told Kelvin to bugger off, demanded his door be released and once it had been, climbed back out of the cab, thumping it on the roof as he did so like a person slapping a stallion on its backside to get it going.

"Fuckwit," Kelvin hollered through the window before pedalling the metal and then sending a red alert voice text to all other local Black cab drivers advising them under no circumstances to give a ride to the bloke whose picture they would soon be picking up on their monitors. After that he sent the pic he'd taken while Norman was flipping his third finger at Sir Keith Staniford.

"He's called Gubbins," said Kelvin, who'd only just remembered the name. "He's Junkett's arse licker and brainwasher. Up to you if you like that kind of person, but I for one *don't*."

Neither, as it turned out, did any of the other drivers in the Black cab family, all of them in one way or the other disgusted by Junkett and his puppet cabinet and many of them returning to the Labour Party under Sir Keith's new leadership. And so it was that Norman was flashed, hooted at, and flipped the finger by eleven Black cabs until finally he realised he must somehow have become a pariah amongst the cabbie fraternity. It wasn't a realisation he allowed into his head easily, mind you. A lot of spitting teeth and foot stamping needed to happen first.

But no good waiting on the pavement outside Sir Keith's secret Chelsea address forever, Norman eventually concluded. So how *else* was he to get back to Kentish Town and pick up the parked Winnebago before heading to his next destination? Buses and tube trains were out of the question. For fear of being contaminated by the great unwashed, Norman had never taken public transport in his whole life and didn't intend to start now the little people were probably all walking, talking, sneezing, coughing, Covid carriers. No, no, no, no, *NO*.

And so it was that a furious and humiliated Norman Gubbins was left with the only option of *walking* all the way from Chelsea back to Kentish Town. Along the way, he tried a few more cabs, but they must have heard the news, too, and just hooted at him or, in the case of the one driven by Barry Kelly, stopped for long enough for Barry to flip a V-sign through the window, then drive off again. *Never* in Norman Gubbins' experience had the little people been so damned petulant and uppity.

"What the hell is wrong with this country?" he asked himself as he stumbled along. Not, you will note, "What the hell is wrong with *me*?" Such are the delusions of hubris.

~ * ~

In 10 Downing Street, and during occasional daring visits to Parliament to bluster and blether about his latest failed Covid policy, Bruno Junkett was experiencing little or no relief from the specialist hospital treatment supposedly guaranteed to fix his deflated left buttock. On some occasions, it would without prior warning *in*flate to twice the size of the right one, and on others it would let out a long hiss—often mistaken by amused bystanders for a fart—before reducing back to the size of a proper Italian thin crust pizza base. All of which meant Bruno still had no guarantee of how to sit normally. One minute he was lopsided to the right, the next to the left and no amount of tactical leg crossing could disguise the wibbly-wobbliness or occasional flatulence. Rupert Splinsky was pleased with these outcomes as he saw them evinced during Commons' PMQs and heard the titters echoing around the Covid-decimated cohort of members. A good job indeed he'd done on the PM.

But parliamentary amusement was the more or less manageable side of Bruno's problem. It was the internationally viral guffaws unleashed by JawJaw's bottom blast lavatory (Lav-a-Tory) explanation of "half-arsed" that shook the PM to the quick, far exceeding the imagination of any inbred ex-Eton and Oxford triumphalist, especially when the story emerged from its social media roots and hit the conventional media headlines all around the globe. Across the political spectrum, the British press revelled in the tale, especially in their cartoon sections, where images of Bruno's naked semi-bottom featured largely as a metaphor for his footling failure to knock Covid on the head as Churchillianly as he had initially declared. Given his vainglorious role in the Brexit fiasco, it was also the Europeans who took pleasure in the discomfiture of *Monsieur Demi-Cul, Herr Halb Arsch, Signor Metà Culo*, as he came to be known and cackled at in France, Germany and Italy to name but three of the most amused nations, although in the Kremlin even the normally lugubrious Igor Ripyurpanzov chuckled. As did the Dougal Klank in the White House, despite his previous declaration that Bruno was "my kinda guy." He'd be laughing on the other side of his orange-painted face the day he found himself testing positive for the virus he, like Junkett, had poo-pooed until far too many people had died of it. But that's the power of nemesis for you.

*Any*way, the folk to benefit most from Junkett's bottom were Enrique and Ramona Schmidt, who were delighted at both the political fallout from this global response to their Bruno's bottom bot and, even more importantly, at the quadrupling of JawJaw's net stock market worth in only six days after its release. Delighted, too, was the deep throat behind the whole enterprise, although Rupert Splinsky kept his delight tactfully to himself except during midnight bottom-of-the-garden telephone chats with sister Ramona.

By contrast, of course, Junkett didn't profit at all from the situation, didn't even draw a percentage from his image being printed on each sheet of a new brand of Tory-blue toilet roll beneath the logo *WATCH YOUR ARSE*, which sold out in supermarkets nationwide after only two days of its release. Okay, all sorts of other toilet rolls were in demand too—mainly for potentially infected surface wiping—because of the latest spike in Covid, but none came anywhere close to the Bruno bum wad, which was *not* the sort of publicity a sitting—okay semi-sitting—prime minister needed in his darkest hour, not at all it wasn't. The bally bug wasn't giving up, and kept on inconveniently killing folk despite the lockdowns in northern towns and cities whose names Bruno kept forgetting. And now *this*! Giggling, pointing, and rib tickling wherever he went.

"What the hell have I done to de*serve* this?" he would moan, writhing in his bed night after night at 10 Downing Street, and thereby irritating his live-in lover/fiancée and waking the baby.

"Been born," would have been the existential answer to Junkett's question as illustrated in the lines of the old Welsh rugby song, "Why was he born so beautiful, why was he born at all? He's no fucking use to any one, he's no fucking use at all." Not that Bruno was much of a rugger bugger at either Eton or Oxford, however much he boasted of his prowess on those fields.

"Poor me, poor *dear* me," he would whimper, tossing and turning to find a more comfortable position, pointlessly because every time he rolled onto his temperamental left buttock, he risked not only the farting noise but also slithering out of bed onto the floor, an accident that had already occurred fourteen times, thereby ranking it as an accident waiting to happen again and again. It was as a result of such midnight mayhem that his live-in lover/fiancée and her baby opted for quieter accommodation next door at number eleven Downing Street, although Bruno barely noticed their absence.

"Who in Gawd's name *did* this to me?" he would continue to bleat on successive nights, but of course nobody, let alone God, had the answer to that question, although it was pretty clear monster mosquitos were still the least likely suspects.

"And where the *hell* is the turncoat Gubbins when I need him most?" he would groan, plumping up his pillow in yet a further fruitless attempt at the sweet oblivion of sleep.

~ * ~

The answer to Bruno's question as to Norman's whereabouts was: he was on his way to a copse of old oaks on Hampstead Heath whither he had wandered after losing his bearings north of Camden Town and taken several wrong turnings. Well, not so much having *lost* his bearings as having been unconsciously lured away from them by the elf Mordecai and his metamorphic dog Hazchem, semi-retired residents of a Vegan hill farm overlooking Derwent Water in the Lake District, who had been recently so disturbed by Brexit, the out-of-control pandemic, and sundry other governmental failures as to require a visit down to London. For many millennia, the pair had done their best to alert humans—kings, queens, dictators, other oligarchs—to the madness in their minds and thereby avert wars and suchlike catastrophes, sometimes with success and sometimes without, and had hoped now was the time to take a well-earned rest on their farm. But you know how it is with elves...how, when yet again faced with human foolishness, they step up to the plate to see how they might help out. Well, okay, probably you *don't* know, but then not a lot of people are ready to suspend their disbelief when it comes to elves, so you'll just have to take my word for it.

Anyway, any*way*, believe it or believe it not, Mordecai and Hazchem *were* of faerie descent, hence their interest in Mister Norman Gubbins, to whom Mordecai accredited much of the populist mayhem that had blighted the green and pleasant land since the Brexit vote of 2016 and thereafter the carelessness for human life but compulsion to preserve the economy written all over Bruno Junkett's early 2020 struggles with Covid. Okay, these were later to be counterbalanced by devil-may-care government spending on furloughs and vaccine development, of which John Maynard Keynes himself would have wholeheartedly approved, but by then over one hundred thousand citizens would already be dead, giving England the unenviable reputation of the nation with one of the highest mortality rates in developed economies. Like Rupert Splinsky, Mordecai was appalled.

"How," he asked Hazchem over a shared pipe of FairyBac on the eve of their imminent teleportation south, "can humans be stupid enough to believe it's possible to have a healthy economy without healthy people to feed it?"

"Raaf, raaf," Hazchem agreed, sprawled in collie form by an open fire.

Mordecai laughed. "I'll take that for agreement."

"Spot on, Mordy," said Hazchem, morphing momentarily into a Superman-type human. Flexing muscles and all that. "So, what do you propose we do about it?"

"Speak persuasively to the person most responsible for counselling such criminality with the hope of setting out a new path for him and his lousy advice before it is far too late. You and I know well enough coronavirus is not going away, but like so many bugs, merely goes on cocking snooks at virologists and politicians by perpetual mutation. This is something that *must* be understood."

"By 'person most responsible,' it's PM Junkett, I presume you mean. He's the one we should speak to?"

"I wish, Hazza, but there would be no point. The man *is* as empty-headed and half-arsed as the current stories suggest, the classically tragic clown figure transgressing all normal social norms to raise either a laugh or tears, just so long as he finds favour. Hence the funny hair and permanent smirk that can equally well elicit smiles or pity.

"So if not him then...?"

"His most recent puppet master, the one who pulled the strings and told him how better to play the game by occasionally pretending to be in earnest. As we know from our little researches"—elves have computer resources that humans don't—"he it was who was responsible for the lavatory bottom dart before running away in a fit of pique, and he therefore who now needs to be persuaded to regain his master's ear, but this time with a fundamentally different message from the previous populist eyewash Junkett came to depend on. Do you see my point, Hazza?"

"Indeed I do, Mordy."

Which was how it came to pass that, after some further discussion and another shared pipe of FairyBac, it was agreed the pair should teleport themselves south, and how it was they should now be awaiting the arrival of Norman Gubbins in the copse of old oaks on Hampstead Heath.

"Mister Gubbins, I presume," said Mordecai by way of introduction, as Norman stumbled into the copse still under the influence of the elf come-hither spell cast upon him which, with a flick of Mordecai's fingers and the muttering of the Spoonerism "Hum Kither," returned Norman to something resembling reality.

"Ugh, um, who're *you*?" he said, rubbing his eyes and then peering at the two strangers, who had morphed for the occasion into tall humans dressed in pin-striped black suits over sparkling white, starched-collar shirts with green cravats.

"You can think of us as friends," said Hazchem, in his *basso profundo* voice.

"Helpers on the long, winding, and oft pitted road," Mordy added. "Oh, and by the way, just to be absolutely clear up front, we know what nobody else appears to know, namely that it was *you* who planted the dart in Bruno Junkett's PM-only water closet facility, thereby causing him to be ridiculed both nationwide and internationally as 'half-arsed'."

Norman gawped. "Huh-huh-*how*..."

"Could we know that?"

"Yuh-yuh-*yes*."

"For you to wonder and us to know," said Hazchem, who wasn't about to disclose to this bozo details of the EIH (Elf Information Highway) that rendered earthlings' cherished satellite and computer-generated images and data little more than child's play.

Mordecai nodded. "Just let's say a reliable source, shall we?"

Out of his depth and on his way to going out of his mind, too, Norman took to scratching his bottom with one hand while pinching his lips with the other. "And what?" he eventually managed to splutter from within the worst dream of his life so far, "are you going to do, whoever you are? Sell me down the river and hang me out to dry?"

At which Mordy and Hazchem shook their heads, mainly in sadness at Gubbins' choice of past-their-sell-by-date clichés, but also in denial of his worst fears.

"We would not so demean ourselves," said Mordy, "although I can well see where such an assumption would come from. Such is the nature of your world."

"*My* world. You mean politics, whoever the bloody hell you are?"

"Actually no, my colleague meant the human world in general," said Hazchem, looking to lighten the atmosphere but inviting instead a warning frown from Mordecai. Hardly likely this clown would figure them for elves, but no chance was worth taking.

And Norman wasn't all that far off in his response. "And you're from fairyland, right?" he said, screwing his thumbs into his temples and waggling the other fingers about. "So why don't you just fuck off back there and let me be on my way? I've enough problems at the moment without dealing with nutters," he added, making to push past Mordecai and Hazchem, who grinned foolishly for the femtoseconds it took them to re-morph into the sort of absurd image humans continue to associate with fairies—dwarfs with green clothes and hair—then in the bat of an eyelid return to their newly chosen human selves.

Which was when, understandably, Norman shrieked, fell to his knees, pummelled the grassy earth for a bit and then fainted. And there we shall leave him as Mordy magicked to their assistance an army tent replete with sufficient medical and other supplies until the following morning when he and Hazchem would have a protracted attempt at alerting him to the misguided beliefs of his benighted ex-master before leaving Norman alone in the copse to reflect on matters and hopefully re-direct his energies and ambitions.

Thirteen

The news of Dougal Klank's positive Covid-19 diagnosis and brief hospitalisation divided public opinion in America and around the world into roughly four camps. These were:

1) Hillbilly, redneck, and alt-right sycophants, who prayed for their president to be cured and go on protecting the country from the deep-state alliance of the QAnon brotherhood and rabid communists threatening to kill them, eat their children, and destroy the gun-slinging America they cherished.

2) Ethically conflicted Americans, who secretly wanted the bastard to suffer hell's fires while not daring to say so in case wishing death on a person, even one as loathsome as Klank, might rebound and kill *them* instead. Over ninety percent of Americans fear one god or another, remember.

3) A largely silent group of cynics worldwide, who initially reckoned the whole thing to be no more than a carefully choreographed hoax designed for Klank to emerge theatrically from the disease as the gallant hero who had beaten the bug, could then pull in the sympathy vote from all sides and get himself elected again. Even they, however, had to wonder at how many doctors would have had to be bribed to

betray their profession when it came to giving the press details of the symptoms and the treatments and drugs administered.

4) Fence sitters, whose previous indecision on matters Klankian was finally resolved by the suspicion Klank had in any case known of his infection days before his diagnosis but had nonetheless gone around pretending nothing was happening and, like Bruno Junkett in the UK, passed on the bug to many of those around him, including his wife and son, White House staff, and the guards in the presidential motorcade he'd insisted on after treatment to prove he was still alive. This was the sort of behaviour that finally made up the vacillators' minds he really was possibly *the* most ego-driven, unempathetic human on the planet, who deserved all he got from Covid-19, especially in light of the going-on nine million cases Klank's administration wasn't lifting a finger to address. Although it couldn't be proven, it seemed likely Jack Bailey's newly increased lead in the polls was down to such sentiments, further reducing Klank's hopes of re-election, largely as the result of this obsession with himself.

Needless to report, the social media exaggerated, distorted, and shuffled all of these attitudes for their own mindless purposes before moving on from Covid, focusing on the coming vital October weeks, and proposing all manner of other tactics Klank might employ to ensure his victory. Most memorable of these came from a Mister X in Kansas City, Missouri, who reckoned hiring a local zoo tiger to eat Jack Bailey could not be ruled out as an option.

Catya Rampersad and Maggie McKenzie, by comparison, bucked all of these trends. They were just royally pissed off at Klank's timing.

"What does he *do* just when we've got all our ducks in a row to make him bald?" said Catya Rampersad to Maggie McKenzie and Hank O'Henry as the trio again sat outside their Penn Ave. Starbucks drinking coffee and smoking cigarettes.

"Goes and catches fucking Covid," said Maggie.

"Or not," said Hank, whose charade suspicions were still in the mix, despite the spread of infection throughout a now barely functioning White House.

"You still figure he was *faking* it?" said Catya.

Hank shrugged. "I'm as confused as the next guy. Everyone knows the creep can't tell the difference between fact and fiction, so why start now?"

"And you don't think he'll need a quick haircut in the meantime?" said an ever-hopeful Maggie. "I can wear a mask and a visor and any other PPE shit necessary."

Hank laughed. "Damn glad you're on my team, babe. I sure would hate for you to be on anybody else's. But the way things stand, nobody but *no*body except his doctor gets near the asshole without mega-clearance. Also, real Covid or fake news Covid, I don't want any pal of mine near that guy right now."

"I read you," said Catya, who had always kept Klank at six arms' lengths anyway in case he ever tried grabbing *her* pussy, and was these days mainly out of the building on "urgent canvassing business."

"And you, Hank? You keeping well clear?"

"You betcha. I got tested and I'm clean."

"Great to hear it. Me, too."

Maggie shook her head. "Must've have been so hard for you guys while everybody around Klank started dropping like flies."

Hank nodded. "It was, but me and Cat kept wearing our masks and washing our hands, didn't we, honey?"

"We sure did. Caught shit from Mister Dougal Denial for it, but who cared."

"And you know what the situation is now?" Maggie continued. "Last I heard was how grrr*eat* the shitkicker was feeling after his treatment, like he was twenty years younger. How he'd been to the real school and learnt his lessons without reading any books. Which as it happens was pretty much the same as his *actual* education. How he beat Covid before it beat him. How it was a gift from God. How fear was just a state of mind. How true Americans should follow his example."

"Right," said Hank. "Superman written all over it. Did you see that picture of him on the White House balcony looking like he was Mussolini or Julius Caesar or somebody?"

Maggie nodded. "Only also looking like he was held up by wires."

"But then even Fox News went silent," said Catya. "Your guess, Hank?"

"Not because no news is good news, that's for sure. Because whatever the hell is happening in the East Wing is being kept under wraps until some new hero story can come out."

Maggie wiped a *faux* tear from her left eye. "So no coiffeuring on the agenda for me any time soon. Even heroes need haircuts, though, don't they?"

"I get any word on that, you'll be the first to know," said Hank. "Now how about I fetch you ladies top-ups? Yours a flat white, Cat, and yours an Americano, Maggie?"

"*You're* the hero around here, Hank," the ladies chorused.

Well, not so much 'chorused.' Catya took the lead and Maggie followed.

~ * ~

Having learnt nothing from Norman Gubbins about the causes of Bruno Junkett's bottom injury, let alone its perpetrator, Sir Keith Staniford was astonished when, back in his House of Commons Leader of the Opposition office, he found the answer to the first of his concerns splashed all across the media. From its roots in JawJaw, a site to which he subscribed no more than he ever had to Facebook or Twitter or any of the other "gasbag" media he detested for their vapid opinionation and blatant lack of legal regulation, it had spread to all sorts of *bona fide* media organs of the kind Sir Keith more or less trusted. Okay so that made him something of a twenty-first century Luddite geek, but he didn't care.

"Bloody hell," he said, scrolling through the articles on his computer and, given his eidetic memory, suddenly out of nowhere recalling Norman Gubbins' hastily covered-up line in their conversation, "I didn't go to the bloody toilet with him, if that's what you're getting at."

"Mmm, I wonder..." Sir Keith was musing as, without a knock on the door or the door even opening, he sensed another presence in his office and, looking round, was greeted by two tall men dressed in pin-striped black suits over sparkling white, starched-collar shirts with green cravats who introduced themselves as notable international journalists.

Well, as you can imagine, as a Yorkshire-born high-profile lawyer and committed adherent to rationalism for all explanations of everything, Sir Keith had *no* time for even a hint of the possibility of preternatural events, especially as evinced in Hollywood movies, and was pretty gobsmacked at this sudden and inexplicable apparition. But even so, he went for the reasonable elucidation of the phenomenon.

"Erm, excuse me, didn't hear you come in. Do we have an appointment?" he said. "Apologies if we do. I was a little distracted with the old computer. Catching up on the news and so on. Possibly it was that which affected my concentration levels."

Mordecai smiled. He liked the cut of this fellow's jib and had taken particular pleasure from his clinically humiliating assaults on Bruno Junkett's waffled replies to his precise questions in Parliament. The disbelief in the extraordinary was understandable and forgivable, so he knew introductions would need to be civil, diplomatic, and quintessentially *human*. No hint of fairydom of the kind they had inflicted on Norman Gubbins must there be.

"Just let me check with my PA," said Sir Keith, picking up his intercom then, when it answered, saying, "No gentlemen in pin-striped suits with green cravats, Malcolm? That's strange, because there are two of them with me in here now. You're *quite* sure you weren't out on a comfort break or something?"

"No, honestly, Sir Keith. Been here all the time working on your conference speech."

Mordy and Hazchem exchanged furtive glances that carried manifold ocular meanings interpretable only to elves. Maybe for once in their lives they had made a boo-boo by not checking in with Malcolm first. You know how it is when you get used to the convenience of teleportation, and forget the niceties of human intercourse. But this meant even civility, diplomacy and suchlike were pretty much out of the window, and other means, fairy ones, would be required to win and sustain Staniford's attention without his calling the police. Top of the list came their special "trust dust" which, when released invisibly into the atmosphere, was guaranteed to suspend its target's disbelief for as long as necessary without doing any damage at all to its inhaler's sensorium in either short or longer terms. How wonderful it would have been if the discovery of a Covid-19 vaccine had been left to elves.

"Ex*treme*ly odd," Sir Keith was saying, as Mordy inched the syringe from his jacket pocket, muttered the word "looportrex" and let fly the mere couple of puffs which, within seconds, would see Sir Keith forget his suspicions and begin smiling broadly before inviting the two "gentlemen" to sit with him around his desk and state their business.

Gesturing Mordy and Hazchem to their seats, he added, "But before we do, perhaps tea or coffee would be in order? With Hobnobs perhaps?"

"*Much* appreciated," said Mordy, with a warning glance at Hazchem who in canine mode was a fool for Hobnobs—drooling, sitting up and begging, all that kind of thing—which during a crucial interview in the office of the Leader of the Opposition in the Mother of Parliaments was the *last* thing they needed.

Hazchem sent him a glance back, which read, "You think I could be so dumb?"

Which, on a number of occasions over the millennia, Hazchem *had* been, but Mordy just smirked meaningfully and let it pass while Sir Keith's PA came in with the refreshments trolley, said hi to the guests, and dispensed the potables and comestibles. You will note that Malcolm was a male PA as opposed to the normal female in such a role. Such were Sir Keith's principles when it came to gender discrimination, meaning not only did blokes do girls' jobs but girls also did blokes'.

And so it was that, masquerading as high-ranking media correspondents from an unnamed foreign country—Fairyland surely *not*—Mordy and Hazchem explained to an eagerly listening Sir Keith how, while in London to explore the tantalizing "Half-Arsed Bruno" story rife in their land, they had quite unexpectedly run into a chap called Norman Gubbins who had turned out to have been Junkett's chief adviser.

"I'm sure you will have heard of him," said Hazchem, succeeding in not drooling while munching a Hobnob.

"Indeed," said Sir Keith. "As a matter of fact, I was talking to him only recently."

"As he told us," said Mordy.

"Gosh. And how was it you ran into him?"

"Serendipity," said Hazchem. "A chance encounter while we were out walking on Hampstead Heath. All we had to do was press him a little and he was happy to talk."

"Impressed by our international credentials," said Mordy.

"Lucky you. My conversation with him was not nearly as productive, I'm afraid. Possibly I pushed him too hard on the matter of Junkett's bottom. I suspected, however, and still suspect, he knew more than he was letting on. But then he pretended to fall ill and got away with the ploy, more fool me."

Aware of this scene from close perusal of their Elf Information Highway monitor, Mordy nodded. "Unfortunate."

"Indeed," said Sir Keith, dunking a Hobnob in his coffee then sucking at it, which caused Hazchem to grab another for himself and try the same trick.

"Funnily enough, however, only moments before you chaps arrived, I was recalling a slip of the tongue, Freudian possibly, in which Gubbins said he didn't go to the toilet with Junkett."

Mordy hoisted an eyebrow. "Is...that...*so?*" he said, although of course he already knew that from EIH, as he also knew of Gubbins' role in the Ripyurpanzov bottom blast narrative.

"Yes," Sir Keith confirmed. "Why would he have said that, one wonders?"

"Clearly a complex character," said Hazchem through megasucks on his dunked Hobnob, which caused Mordy to raise a warning eyebrow.

"No question about it," Sir Keith agreed.

"Who is now prepared for a re-run of your last encounter," said Mordy, for this was the agreement the elves had reached with Norman after the protracted Hampstead Heath copse morning conversation in which, with the addition of a few drops of a special pink elf potion called "ethikos" to his morning tea, they had outlined to him their disquiet in face of the populist political devices over recent years employed by Klank in the USA and Junkett in the UK to hurl wrecking balls at representative democracy.

In that last encounter in particular, Mordy had emphasised his disgust at the narcissism implicit in such leaders' post-election me-me-mine posturing. What *royally* pissed off both him and his colleague Hazchem, however, were the snide, self-serving subterfuges of the *éminences grises* behind such monsters of anti-democratic depravity. To emphasize this point, Hazchem had morphed into a disgruntled Wolfhound and snapped at Norman's ankles, causing him to cringe.

"Unfair treatment," I hear you object. "Brainwashing with the threat of physical harm."

Very possibly, but take a moment to reflect, if you will, on the "fairness" of worldwide dispensations that function beneath the whims of crackpot, inevitably male, rulers. Think the despots who run the Middle East here. Think Ripyurpanzov, who plans to rule Russia until he dies. And, of course, Junkett and Klank.

*Any*way, even after the ethikos had worn off, the self Norman Gubbins returned to was a self far from the normal one. Unlike Sam Bundy, he hadn't experienced an epiphany in which he went crazy, jabbered insanely, and saw himself as one of Eliot's hollow, stuffed men, but the truth factor in the arguments Mordy and Hazchem had prosecuted were hard to deny. Shall we just say it was an unusually *humbled* Norman who had found his head nodding at aspects of the elves' presentation, as if something radical had happened to pierce the defences of his previously unexamined *amour propre*. Distantly from his Oxford PPE days, he recalled Socrates's dictum that the unexamined life wasn't worth living, and there was no way he could pretend *his* life had been examined beyond its naked compulsion to power.

That was when Hazchem had morphed back into human form and asked if Norman would care to admit it had been he who planted the dart that shot Bruno Junkett in his left buttock because he hadn't been put forward for a career-crowning knighthood.

"You *know* about that?" Norman had asked, but not aggressively.

"Yes, as we told you last night," replied Mordy. "We elves have our ways and means."

"Uh huh," said Norman, as if this were now a perfectly understandable claim. "And how do you guys feel I should move on from here?"

Which was when Mordy had suggested firstly a return discussion with Sir Keith Staniford to see if any common ground might still be found, and secondly some serious bridge-mending with Bruno Junkett to help alter his so far rubbish coronavirus policies.

"But Staniford's a *socialist*," was the programmed riposte on the very tip of Norman's tongue, but somehow it didn't get air space. Instead, he had just nodded. "Okay, why not?"

"Why not indeed?" said Mordy, "Let us see if that might be arranged, shall we?"

It was of the essence of that conversation with Norman—minus any reference to elvish insights into his doings—that Mordy informed Sir Keith, who agreed readily enough to such a proposal. "Of course, my door is always open. And how did you chaps manage such a transformation?" he asked.

"A case of you to wonder, us to know," said Mordy. "But you may just find you will get an answer to your suspicion of Gubbins having had something to do with Junkett's explosive toilet experience. Good luck with that."

Which was when Sir Keith found himself alone in his office again. Why? Because that was also when Mordy whispered "xertropool," the reverse of the magic word "looportrex," and he and Hazchem re-teleported themselves and vanished, leaving Sir Keith alone with his computer.

"Mmm, strange," he muttered to himself. Yet lodged in his cerebrum was the possibility of a further, and possibly fruitful, encounter with Norman Gubbins. Quite how or why this had come to pass he wasn't exactly sure but, thanks to Mordy's little potions, for once in his lawyerly life, he wasn't minded to disentangle such arcane conundrums.

Fourteen

Unlike a number of previous famous patients at Harvard Medical School's McLean psychiatric hospital, in bed thirteen, ward ten of that institution, Sam Bundy wasn't making a whole lot of progress when it came to shucking off the paranoid psychosis with which he had been diagnosed. Mind you, it might have been wiser for the renowned consultant psychiatrist Professor Horst Schnitzenthaler *not* to have allowed Sam to watch Dougal Klank's triumphal return to the election trail in Florida after supposedly having been cured of the coronavirus he may or may not have had. Had Sam instead been persuaded to become a fan of *Kipo and the Age of Wonderbeasts*, for example— always assuming he didn't associate Klank as one such—he might not have hurled the bottle of Ziprasidone at the TV and smashed the screen. But that's shrinks for you, always thinking they know the far end of everything...in this instance, Schnitzenthaler reckoning he'd spotted Sam's need to confront his demons, in which case his proposed cure was about as therapeutic as advising an arachnophobe to watch spiders mating. And matters certainly were not improved by Schnitzenthaler's lack of empathy when it came to the shattered TV.

"The fuck did you have to go and do *that* for?" he upbraided Sam, which was tantamount to a general practitioner asking a patient what the matter with him was today, to which the rational response would be, "That's what I came to you to find out, Doc."

Sadly for Schnitzenthaler, however, despite remaining furious at Klank's obscene posturing before a massed throng of unmasked, anti-socially distanced Covid deniers and potential QAnon believers, Sam still retained the woozy acumen to spot this aporia in clinical good practice, which was how come he leapt from his bed, socked Horst on the nose, then took to tugging at his ears and sticking out his tongue.

It was hardly surprising at this juncture in his treatment that Sam should have been removed from McLean and sent instead to a detention centre for unapologetic recidivists hidden amidst Coney Island's otherwise fun-loving tourist provisions. After all, the guy still had a five-million-dollar bail bond hanging over his head and needed a secure environment ahead of his trial, in case he did anything further to blot his copybook and thereby prejudice the jury's verdict on his misdoings. Which copybook blotting, irrespective of legal outcomes, Sam achieved on day one of his new incarceration by going stir crazy, biting a warden, and being committed to indefinite solitary confinement, where he went even stir crazier.

Anyway, *any*way, so much for the most recent update on Sam Bundy. You could almost feel sorry for the guy, couldn't you? Well, *al*most.

~ * ~

Far more deserving of sympathy were the millions of folk on the planet whose sanity was currently being challenged to its limits by the failure of their governments to agree on appropriate methods to protect them from the Covid virus that either existed or didn't, depending on who you listened to. Prime amongst these were, of course, the Americans whose soon-to-be-ex-president and his flat-earth followers reckoned the bug was only a myth and all Klank had been suffering from was flu *but* whose top scientists were telling folks to wear masks and stay home or die. Which of these beliefs was true, they wanted to know, until they ended up in hospital or the crematorium. It was the same story with Brazil's Bolsonaro and other nutjob populist leaders around the globe, including the UK's Junkett, who kept on promising paradise further down the road, while vacillating between lockdowns one minute and openings up the next, thereby confusing (and infecting) even more people.

Yet, even in sensible countries whose leaders took the scientific advice seriously and staged strictly enforced restrictive policies to stem the flow of disease before it became a flood, citizens became restless locked up in their homes and took to partying illegally in the streets late at night and to hell with face masks, hand-washing, social distancing and all the rest of the bullshit. These were the same folks who would flood the Internet with Covid denial messaging, in the process bursting whatever dams there were in place to inhibit even more infections. Put simply, even some of the once sanest people went batshit crazy, proclaiming they'd prefer to take their chances and have their old lives back, thank you very much, the most cynical of them claiming they were doing it for the sake of helping the economy. Hence the fuck-you-Junkett raves out in the countryside when yet again all the pubs, restaurants, and other public places were under severe restrictions because Bruno had so decreed for want of anything better to decree. Which had *also* pissed off all those publicans and restaurateurs who would soon lose their livelihoods, and infuriated local mayors who wanted proper financial compensation for such losses, thus giving rise to unseemly bickering, especially between the northern provinces and Westminster at the very moment national solidarity was most needed. And so it went, on...and on...and *on*. U-turns every five minutes such that nobody knew what the fuck was going on. Meanwhile, the mortality rate kept rising and hospitals went on overflowing unchecked by the likes of double-dealing Junkett and brain-dead Klank. In short, across the globe, folk were going pretty much as crazy as Sam Bundy. And this was still late 2020 remember, back in the BV (Before Vaccines) era.

Meanwhile, Monseigneur Covid was grinning all over his spikey face.

"Yummy, yummy, yummy in my tummy," he said, watching on as human leaders wherever he looked were so satisfyingly screwing up and knowing full well that even in the PV (Post Vaccines) years he'd still be able to mutate often enough to muddy their waters for the foreseeable future—with any luck forever.

~ * ~

Back in the tranquillity of their Lake District farmhouse after the London visit, Mordecai and Hazchem shook their heads in as much dismay as elves can muster, given elves are *nil desperandum* types to the core of their eternal beings.

"What on Earth can we do to help?" asked Mordy. "Even *we* appear to be out of our depth against such odds. Trying to re-brand Gubbins was only a drop in the ocean."

Hazchem nodded. "We could contact Phoebe the Future Fairy to see how things pan out in the end."

You will recall that elves exist in a timeless present with only flashes of memory of the past and little inclination to predict the future beyond tomorrow, hence their wisdom. Phoebe was the *only* one exempt from these drawbacks, but for fear of exhaustion required she should only be contacted *in extremis*.

"No, we must respect her rights," said Mordy. "And she is only a broad-brush forecaster, after all."

"True enough," said Hazchem, morphing for comfort into a Golden Retriever and stretching out in front of the log fire.

Mordy twiddled his age-old beard. "It's not even as though *we* can offer them the pesticide they need. I would sooo love to but..."

And Mordy was right, not just because he and Hazchem didn't have access to hi-tech laboratories, but also because fairies have no first-hand experience of deadly disease or indeed death itself, and therefore no need to have developed the means to prevent them. Yes, they had potions of many kinds to alleviate transitorily unhelpful conditions, but that was about the size of it. And also yes, while Fairyland had never been an entirely peaceful place, given the occasional internecine squabbles featuring boggarts in particular, nonetheless these had always been resolved by recourse to the above-mentioned potions plus dancing and singing. When it came to humans, however, it was a whole different story—lifetimes filled with pride, the necessary lies to protect it, and then a sad slippage into old age and expiry, "Sans teeth, sans taste, sans eyes, sans everything" as Jacques describes the condition in *As You Like It*.

Hazchem turned his toes towards the fire and sighed his agreement with this analysis. "No getting away from it."

"Sooo," Mordy concluded. "Is there *any*where we can look to add a little grain of hope to the human condition as it currently stands in this the year of their lord twenty-twenty?"

"I have one little idea," said Hazchem.

"Shoot," said Mordy.

Which was how it came to pass that Catya Rampersad and Maggie McKenzie finally came to appreciate how much in love with each other they were. Call it an epiphany, call it mystical intervention, call it anything you want, but there was no denying the suddenness with which Mordy's spell—for that's what it was—hit them. One moment they were sitting on a sofa watching CBS evening news in Catya's Columbia Heights apartment and, like Sam Bundy, contemplating hurling objects at the screen, as during a town hall debate Klank gurgled inchoately in response to perfectly simple questions, the next moment, bammo, just like that, they were naked in bed together. And what we're talking here was not the cheap porno sex of the kind peddled all across the Internet…this was sex springing from a passion that could be expressed no other way. Language certainly wouldn't have carried nearly the same meaning as tongues used for very different purposes.

"Holy shit," said Catya, when the first impact was over and the pair lay intertwined beneath tangled sheets. "Where did *that* come from?"

Maggie shook tousled hair from her eyes. "I guess it's been brewing a while but we never dared admit it."

"It was magic though, huh?" said Catya, with no concept of how accurate her comment was.

"You can say that again, babe. Only we tell no one, right?"

"Wrong. We tell *every*one. Klank or no Klank these are also LGBT days. Me, I am gonna get a Gay Pride Covid mask."

Maggie laughed. "Yeah, okay, get me one, too. I'll wear it when I cut the asshole's hair. Whenever *that* will be."

Catya sighed. "Let's leave the politics out of this for the moment, honey. If it happens, it happens. If it doesn't, it doesn't. Meanwhile..." she said massaging Maggie's right nipple, "You wanna have another go-around at this?"

And Maggie did. For the record it was two forty-five a.m. by the time they'd had their fourth go-around and collapsed into dreamless sleeps.

"Raaf, *raaf*," Hazchem enthused, not from any perverse interest in lesbian sex, because elves are androgynous and have never much minded who does what to whom or why. No, no, because it was just so great to see at least *two* humans so together and so contented in a world so riven with discontents.

"Indeed, old chap. A *jolly* good idea you had," Mordy agreed. "Now, how about a pipe of FairyBac before we also turn in?"

"With pleasure," said Hazchem, morphing back into a regular elf and heading for the FairyBac cupboard wherein lay little bottles containing a wide variety of tobacco-like substances all starting from a base of the elvish version of marijuana. "Nothing like a little oblivion, eh?"

Mordy smiled. "Needed now more than ever."

Whether Catya Rampersad *really* dreamed of an elf band playing Paul Simon's song "Bridge Over Troubled Water" that night will forever remain a mystery, but Maggie McKenzie swore that was the tune her lover was humming when she awoke the following morning.

Fifteen

Up his lazy Mississippi creek, Silas Baudoin was feeling pretty much as desperate about the human condition as Mordy and Hazchem, but without the magical resources to do even the smallest thing about it. Time and again, he swore to himself he would allow his smartphone's battery to run dry so he would never again be tempted to hear of the mayhem in the outside world, but if he did that, there would be no more contact with the family, particularly Catya, sooo... so time and again when the charge dipped, he plugged the phone into the sole source of electricity in his cabin, a socket by his bed that led to God only knew where. Silas had never asked when his nephew Matthias had insisted on installing it, or else all deals were off when it came to allowing his uncle to continue his solitary existence.

"What if you get sick?" Matthias said as he fiddled with wires. "What then? You think the gods of the forest are gonna save you?"

Never having suffered a day's illness in his life, Silas hadn't thought of that, but supposed Mattie was probably right.

"Gonna be damn difficult getting help up here, Uncle Silo, but at least someone will be hearing you if help's needed. All you gotta do is dial nine-one-one, okay?"

"Nine-one-one," Silas repeated dutifully, although what with his memory outages there was every chance the number would soon be history. Song lyrics he could remember from way back—they must have imprinted themselves somehow— but numbers and names were becoming a challenge. He'd tried reminding himself he needed to remember them, but then somehow the reminder got muddled up with a reminder for something *else*—like how today he would need to harvest some forest food for his and Rufus's dinner.

"If you don't keep the battery charged," pesky Mattie had continued, "you won't be able to keep up on what's happening in the world outside."

"True enough," Silas had said. Back then he had wanted to keep up. Right now, he knew only too much of his country's woes. A quarter of a million and counting dead from the Covid, thousands sick and out of work with no health insurance, and all Klank could think about was another term in which to wreak yet more havoc on America's cherished political system in favour of self-glorification.

Still, however hard Silas might try, he couldn't completely shut himself off from the news. It was almost like a compulsion, but not one based on *schadenfreude,* for Silas took no pleasure from other folks' troubles. It was in some entirely altruistic way it troubled him in broadcast after broadcast to hear of the horrors folks were living through while their president sucked his own dick. When the hell was that gal going to cut his hair off after the Bad Bug episode and now with the election only weeks away? This was a question he put to Catya in one of her regular calls.

"Looks like it's on hold for a while," she replied.

"Sorry to hear that," said Silas.

Catya frowned. This wasn't the normally sprightly Uncle Silas down the line. There was something in the voice, something sombre and sad.

"You okay there, Unc?" she said.

"Kinda worn down, if you wanna know, babe. Must be old age catching up with me. The country going down the tubes ain't helping none either."

"Sure. I know where you're coming from, and you all alone down there. None of the family been around to say hello?"

"They can't. There's been some kinda shutdown or lockdown or whatever you call it, so they can't leave the city right now. We talk on the phone sometimes, but they have their lives, right? All I really need to know is they're dodging the bug and getting on with stuff. That keeps me happy enough."

"But don't tell me some company would do you any harm."

Silas couldn't deny it, but saw what Catya was about to suggest. "Sure it wouldn't, honey, but don't...like DO *NOT*...give me no nonsense about you hiking down here to see some old timer stuck up a creek with only a dog to talk with. Rufus is a whole lot more fun than a lot of humans, mind. Give him his dinners and he's happy. There ain't a hurtful bone in his body. This is a guy with no enemies and nothing to prove."

Catya laughed. "That why you let him sleep in your bed with you?"

"Yeah, well there is that to it. He likes the company. And it can get chilly out here nights sometimes. Anyhow *any*how, babe, good talking with you," said Silas, aware he had moaned when he hadn't meant to and keen to cut the call.

But Catya wasn't finished. "Listen up, Unc," she said. "Remember that hair-cutting gal I told you about? Maggie is her name."

"Sure I do."

"And how I'd bring her down to hide out with you when she'd done the job on Klank?"

"Yeah. The pretty gal who'd probably get bored around an old guy like me," said Silas as the lyrics to George Gershwin's "It Ain't Necessarily So" unaccountably sprang to his dicky memory, particularly the lines about Methuselah living nine hundred years, but nobody called that livin' when no gal would give in to no man who was nine hundred years old. This he did not report to Catya in case she thought he gone terminally insane with that crazy old folks' disease— what was its name again? Holzhomers, Alpenheimers, some name like that.

"That's the gal," said Catya. "Well, how about we made that trip anyway?"

"Didn't I just tell you I'm okay, so please don't put yourself out in my behalf? If there's lockdowns here on the Mississippi, there sure as hell must be in D.C."

"Yeah, but I have this special White House pass, right? I say I need to catch an airplane, I can catch an airplane to most any place."

"Holy shit," said Silas.

"Besides, me and Maggie are in a special kind of relationship I'd like to tell you about and like you to see how it works."

"Well, if you figure it's a possibility, babe, then I ain't gonna deny it would be sweet to see y'all."

"I'll get back to you with a date," said Catya. "Meanwhile you take care of yourself, okay?"

"Gonna do my damnedest, honey. And thanks for the little light down the tunnel."

"My pleasure, Unc. Now I've got to love you and leave you. Duty calls and all that."

That night Silas Baudoin slept better than he had for many days.

~ * ~

Once Mordy and Hazchem had done their best to wash Gubbins' mind of its current obsessions, open his eyes to new ways of being and pay a return visit to Sir Keith Staniford, they had taken their leave and Norman had lain back on the copse's verdant covering staring up at a sky that was for once blue, cloudless, and undisturbed by climate change's gusty winds. Normally a restless sleeper, and with-the-dawn riser full of busy-busy-busy cunning subterfuges to occupy the coming day, for possibly the first time in twenty years, he had slept dreamlessly for nine hours and was about to drop off again until tapped on the chest by a Hampstead Heath volunteer ranger/gardener called Barry—"the Barrow Boy" to his friends—who said, "Sorry to disturb you, pal, only you'd best be on your way."

Surprising himself, Norman didn't bicker or bite this bloke's head off as was his custom with insignificant "little people," but just got first to his knees then up on his toes before stretching to the sky and saying, "Nice morning."

Barry smiled. Hampstead Heath was known for its midnight parties and the late sleepers to whom he usually turned a blind eye, but he couldn't ignore London's recent elevation to the third tier—some said "tear"—of Junkett's latest Covid clampdown wheeze with its varying regional restrictions. What if this geezer were a super-spreader? What if he'd tested positive and was running away from being traced? He wasn't wearing a mask, after all. A mess of muddled questions ran through George's mind, unsurprisingly, seeing as such muddledom was pretty much the hallmark of the government's benighted "policies" where the virus was concerned. First one idea, then another, then back to a revised version of the first, then an*other* midnight insight announced the following morning and retracted by mid-afternoon until no sane person was able to keep up with what the hell was going on—except for Mister Coronavirus, that was, who just went on infecting folk regardless (see above).

"So it is," said Barry, in regard to the morning. "Now if you'd care to be on your way, I'd be obliged."

"Fine, wonderful, okay, understood," said an uncharacteristically compliant Norman, who moved to shake Barry's hand and then laughed when the ranger took two apologetic steps backwards and raised his palms to indicate the need for at least two metres of social distancing. "Sorry, sorry," he added. "I forgot."

"Like too many of our fellow citizens, I'm sorry to say, but apologies accepted," said Barry, going for an elbow bump instead.

This was a novel experience for Norman, but one he quite enjoyed. Funny how pleasant such amiable contact could be with a person he would only recently have dismissed as a mindless pleb whose only function in life had been to believe in Norman's algorithmic Brexit slogans like TAKE BACK CONTROL, vote Leave, and ensure the 2016 referendum went the way he and Junkett wanted, which it did, hence his elevation to top 10 Downing Street insider.

By the time he'd stopped thinking those things, however, Barry was already on the other side of the copse busy pruning bushes, so without further ado Norman wandered off, unwittingly in the direction of Kenwood House, a seventeenth-century mansion in its own carefully manicured grounds. Hampstead Heath is nothing like Silas Baudoin's Mississippi creek when it comes to raw natural beauty but, a little like New York's Central Park, it at least offers a green refuge from the craziness of the city that surrounds it. Strawberry Fields forever!

Norman knew nothing about Nature, though. Once, while taking a break from Downing Street in St James's Park, he'd been stopped by a toddler pointing at a mallard wanting to know what it was called and, thinking himself funny, Norman had answered "Johnny," which didn't amused Aileen, the toddler's mother, not at all it didn't.

"What little Ivan meant was what *species* is it," she countered.

That floored Norman, who hurried off, calling over his shoulder, "Duck."

And so it went with the rest of the animal kingdom. Norman knew what dogs, cats, horses, sheep and suchlike looked like, but had no clue as to different breeds of them or any other domestic creatures. And as for *wild* animals, apart from the normal zoo ones, they remained as much of a mystery as the rest of the natural world he had no interest in. Weeping willows he could just about recognize, but as for silver birches, alders and spruces, let alone swamp cypresses and suchlike, they were just "trees." And as for hydrangeas, daffodils, surfinia, myositis, buddleia and all the rest, they were "flowers" or "plants" or maybe both.

Which was a pity, because as he strolled along aware of going nowhere between age-old oaks, an unidentifiable sense of profound relief overcame him. No traffic noise, no hubbub, no shops, none of his beloved signifiers of pre-Covid civilisation, but in some arcane way they no longer seemed to matter, their absence an irrelevance. A pity it was that, suspicious of anybody across The Channel, especially poets, Norman had never come across Charles Baudelaire's poem *Correspondances*, which obviously has greater resonance in French, but to give you an idea, here's an English translation of the most memorable bit.

> "Nature's a shrine where living columns stand
> And now and then breathe a confounded phrase,
> Man wanders there amidst a forestland
> Of symbols, followed by their knowing gaze."

For the francophones amongst you, the far more emotive original is:

"La nature est un temple où de vivants piliers.
Laissent parfois sortir de confuses paroles;
"L'homme y passe à travers des forêts de symboles.
Qui l'observent avec des regards familiers."

The point here being that trees, symbolic or real, live a whole lot longer than us humans and thereby witness all the fuckups we make. A shame we have needed to cut so many of them down to build railways and roads, and who knows maybe it was precisely such deforestation that ushered in Mister Coronavirus. Nature's revenge? Well maybe, but that's a whole different story.

*Any*way, as for Norman Gubbins on his peculiar peregrinations, obviously enough nothing of the kind initially occurred to a blinkered mind like his. But as he approached Kenwood House, the weirdest thoughts began to download themselves, thoughts of peace, harmony, fraternity, and tranquillity. So much so that he needed to sit on a bench overlooking an ancient magnolia tree, let his mind wander and wonder. Not so much about the ancient beauty and wisdom of trees, more about why, for once in his sweet life, he wasn't actually *thinking* at all. It was as if his normally febrile mind had been switched off by some invisible force and he were living a dream in which for once *he* only featured as a peripheral character. Namelessly he drifted through extraordinary scenes in which the folk around him in some unidentifiable landscape were happy. They danced, sang, hugged each other, exchanged presents, and in due course invited him to join them. Which he did, dancing and singing badly but nobody cared, just laughed and hugged him. Afterwards there were drinks and snacks and a princess called Melissa led him away to a castle, across the moat, and to her bedchamber where she was in the course of slowly divesting herself of the many garments and jewels she wore when...

When all of a sudden Norman was awakened by an American voice next to him on the bench barking, "Snap out of it, asshole."

"Uh?" he muttered turning to see a guy with long ratty grey hair and sparse beard.

"You talking to me?" Norman heard himself saying as he peered at the spectral creature which reminded him a lot of Sam Bundy.

"Damn right I am," said Spectral Sam.

"Look, *if* you wouldn't mind..." muttered Norman, making to rise from the bench but finding his legs wouldn't support him and sitting back down.

"I *mind*, Gubbins."

"You know my *name*?"

Increasingly riled, Spectral Sam said, "Are you *kid*ding me? Once we ruled the populist world, you and me, right?"

"We *did*?"

"Sure we did, so quit it with the dreamy dreams and the questions and listen up."

"To what?"

"The heads-up I'm gonna give you."

Norman began to sweat and was sweating a whole more by the time Spectral Sam had run the down the gamut of his rabid predictions about the future failure of the worldwide populist agenda should Klank fail to win back the presidency, of which Spectral Sam reckoned there was every chance.

"Ever since he fired me, he's been heading towards being the loser he's always really been," he asserted, "And lemme tell you, Gubbins, the same is gonna happen to Junkett here in the UK. Back in twenty-sixteen we were winners, am I right?"

Norman nodded. Such glory days *those* had been.

"But this is twenty-twenty and look at you now," Sam persisted. "Another freakin' loser, if you ain't careful. Okay, so you shot Junkett in the ass, hoo-*rah* for that. But where d'you go from there? There're evil forces out there trying to twist your mind around, Gubbins. Like the guys with the snazzy suits and funny ties back in the park?" Sam threw an arm back towards the direction Norman had come from. "The ones who dosed you then fed you fantasies."

Distantly, as if on some other planet, Norman remembered Mordecai and Hazchem.

"Yeah, and?" he said.

"They were agents of the devil and of Deep State. They were sweet-talking dipshits fooling with your mind. Your task on this Earth, Gubbins, is to continue the teaching I gave you. Right now, I can't. I got my own troubles."

Norman nodded again. Like everybody, he'd heard of Bundy's forthcoming lawsuit. Of what had happened to him in the meantime he had no idea. Like what the hell was he doing in London, for example.

"So, Gubbins, I am relying on you not to break with the faith. Remember the will of the people and how to manipulate it if you want the results we both once achieved. Go to the meet-up with the fuckwit Staniford if it makes you feel better. But on *your* terms, not his."

Norman was nodding yet again when suddenly—swoosh, just like that—the space on the bench beside him emptied itself and Spectral Sam was gone.

Never for the remainder of his life would Norman Gubbins be able to understand what had just happened, but for the present of one thing he was now sure, namely not to take any more shit from anyone. Get back to the old Gubbins was the message. Yes, he would go to see Staniford again but, as Spectral Sam advised, only with his own agenda. Meanwhile, he needed to grope his way out of this spooky place and find his way back home, *if* any Black cab would stop for him.

Which once he was out on Spaniards Road one mercifully did. And there was no recognition fuss this time, or any arguing over face coverings. Why? Because hopelessly groping in his coat pocket, he discovered the mask Mordy had planted there in case of such an eventuality. That it had Black Lives Matter written across it a preoccupied Norman understandably did not notice.

It wasn't by coincidence that the cabbie waiting for him was George Ballentine's younger brother Mikey, who had been instructed so to do by Mordy on his Black cab fairy app. Why? Because Mordy and Hazchem had followed Norman's progress to Kenwood House on Elf Information Highway, been pleased by his apparent change of character, then appalled by the Spectral Sam intervention, but nonetheless keen at least to ensure he was safely delivered home without further upset, especially conflict on the race relations front. Hence the Black Lives Matter mask and now Mikey Ballentine, who had also played for the Accies—as a left wing back, if you're interested. Not that Norman noticed the resemblance between the two brothers. Just glad for the absence of hassle, he merely gave Mikey the Kentish Town address, climbed into the cab, lay back, and tried to make any kind of sense at all of the weirdest day of his life so far. Mikey had to wake him up when the short trip was over and, to Norman's astonishment, declared the ride a "freebie."

"What the fuck?" he said.

But Mikey just smiled, tapped his own BLM mask, helped his passenger out of the cab, and drove off, leaving Norman on the pavement to ponder the bizarre circumstance of a Black person being kind to a white person with no trace of payback or servility. More's the pity he didn't ponder long, though, because by the time he awoke the following morning, the experience had been relegated to the waste bin of dreamland as bits of the true Gubbins began to resurface.

And there, sadly, we must leave Mordy's experiment in producing a new Norman.

Sixteen

In the week running up to the American presidential election, Bruno Junkett was still worried by the universal ridicule directed at his faulty bottom and by the absence of his trusted counsellor Norman Gubbins, but even those problems were eclipsed by the image of Dougal Klank touring the USA prating about how Covid-19 would be conquered the very day after he was voted back into the White House. As a constitutional liar from childhood, Bruno was fully aware of the success alternative realities could bring a person, but even he worried about the difference between the advantages of an ordinary lie and the flat-out denial of the WHO's well publicised data showing the exact opposite of what Klank was claiming, given that Covid cases in America currently stood at around nine million. Yet still the Klank-maniacs, especially on the prairies and in the South, gathered in vast numbers at his rallies self-consciously mask-less in tribute to the hero who had survived the illness he may or may not have had, and asserting their rights as true Americans never to be pushed around by anybody, let alone the scientists Klank had tweet-smeared as "idiots." With the backing of such blind pugnacity, he was home free to tell them Covid would be gone the very day after his re-election.

All of which was fine and dandy, the same sort of Gubbins-inspired schtick Bruno had himself used in winning the Brexit referendum by demonising Europeans—Klank's scientists—as enemies from whom true Brits needed to be freed once and for all. This was nice neat lying with a happy outcome, notably when it led to the PM job. But still, conveniently forgetting his own Covid-denial phase, Bruno worried about Dougal losing his grip, and possibly his marbles, by pushing mendacity beyond the limits of the (in)credible. Were he to lose the election, oligarchic populists the likes of Bruno would also lose a vitally important front-running ally in the fight to abolish liberal democracy Ripyurpanzov-style and then centralise power around themselves, while a Jack Bailey win would bolster the popular credibility of socialist and liberal rivals worldwide. Which Bruno did...*not*...want, no siree. What he needed now was a radical switch of storyline, one in which he was no longer mocked for talking through his half-arse, and instead became the heroic darling of the masses. For which chicanery he needed the wiles of Norman Gubbins back in Downing Street and on song. But Norman damn-his-eyes Gubbins had vanished. And it wasn't even as though Bruno could give the matter his full attention, because Mister sodding Coronavirus had inconveniently taken to infecting even more folk than expected and Bruno was supposed to do something about it, like impose another bally lockdown and screw up the economy—to the dismay of the rich—or not to impose any more restrictions and let the bally bug run riot—to the detriment of the poor and fury of hospital staff across the nation. *Not* the sort of choice he expected to be required to make when becoming prime minister. Bruno's idea of leading a country was to be no more than a Klank-style playboy figurehead swanning about the country in search of heroic photo ops while the little people beneath him did whatever work needed doing or got fired for failing.

"Fuck, fuck, fuckity *fuck*," he muttered to himself, sipping at a tumbler of prosecco while scrolling down US media reports of the latest voting figures and their possible relevance to who would win the White House. None of them was conclusive, of course, how could they be? But many, even Fox News, were signalling a whole different ballgame from the 2016 victory. Sure, the solid gun-toting cowboys and hillbillies were still on board, but there was worrying evidence of an abnormally large early voting turnout all across the country. And what if these numbers came from the newly registered young voters with liberal mindsets? Also, what if more of the BLM and BAME communities, surely not Klankites, were to turn up at the polling stations? And then there were the women, and not just those in the House of Representatives, women sick and tired of swinging dick, pussy-grabbing Klank getting his way in the wider world—an eerie reminder to Bruno of his history of philandering and misogyny. Plus, all of a sudden there were the LGBT boys, girls and freaks to take into account.

"God above, how could the world come to this?" Bruno asked himself after a third glass of prosecco.

God had no answer to this question unless you were to interpret as a divine response the sudden *de*flation of Bruno's recently *in*flated left buttock, thereby causing him to tip off his computer chair right on top of 10 Downing Street's cat Moggie, who took her revenge by squirming out from beneath her master and pissing on his head before taking her leave to seek pastures greener. What, Bruno wondered gloomily, climbing to his feet and drying his sodden locks, if Moggie were some dreadful harbinger of similar behaviour from his fellow humans, particularly the Tory grandees who had so recently welcomed his ascent to Downing Street glory, but at the first signs of discontent would be only too happy to ditch a potential loser and if then he were to follow Klank into the political wilderness? It was a sickening concept indeed.

And, as with Norman Gubbins, there, *pro tem*, we shall leave Bruno Junkett and his woes.

~ * ~

Catya Rampersad and Maggie McKenzie flew into Louis Armstrong New Orleans the Saturday before the election and were met at the airport by Silas Baudoin's nephew, Matthias Dupree who, as a senior policeman, had been able to pull some strings to dodge local Covid restrictions and arrange to ferry his cousin and her friend to the cabin up the creek in an NOPD river boat cruiser.

"So great of you gals to come and see the old guy," he said in the meeters and greeters lounge after Catya had introduced him to Maggie as her partner. "This a surprise visit, or does he know you're coming?"

"He knew we'd come, but he didn't know when," said Catya, who'd barely seen her cousin since they'd been kids way back when, and even then only rarely, different branches of the family and all that. Back then Mattie had always been reckoned the naughty boy, but she figured he must have changed big time since becoming a policeman, although she rather hoped not. No way could she imagine *him* buying into police procedures sufficiently to hand down the kind of punishment that suffocated George Floyd.

"That's nice, he's gonna just love seein' y'all. And you and Maggie are podnas in what? And don't tell me crime."

Catya laughed. "Far from it, Mattie. We're partners in love."

An hiatus while Mattie computed this, but then to Catya's and Maggie's surprise and relief he shook his head and smiled. "Congratulations to you both," he said. "What Louisiana and the whole of the US needs right now is a little more love of all kinds. Too much violence and too much of the macho Klank horseshit, am I right?"

Which reply earned Mattie Dupree the pleasure of getting himself hugged harder by two women simultaneously than at any other time in his life so far. Mind you, at no time in his life so far either had he been practically hugged to death by two *mask*-wearing women. It was all pretty spooky, but Mattie got the message.

"Wow*eee*, I gotta say this kinda stuff more often," he said when the hugging was over and he had donned his own NOPD mask in sympathy. "Okay with you guys if we hit the road now? I got the car waiting."

"Great, terrific, this is sooo good of you," said Catya as they headed outside. "You're sure we're not taking up too much of your time?"

"Nah. I took a day's leave and the kids are hunkered down at home doing home schooling with their mom."

"Hurricane Zeta?" said Maggie.

"Yeah. School's closed, power outages and the like. Plus there's the Covid. You're lucky the airport stayed open."

Catya nodded. "And you're sure, sure, sure the river'll be OK?"

Mattie grinned. "Could be a little choppy and bouncy out there, but we'll make it."

Bronx-born Maggie paled a little at the prospect of bouncing about on the Mississippi river and squeezed Catya's hand, but smiled bravely as her lover squeezed back.

"And Uncle Silas?" said Catya. "You checked in with him lately, Mattie?"

"Sure have and he's fine. Some trees came down in the storm, but none on him or the dog Rufus, so yeah, all's good with them. Ookay, so here we are at the limo for the ladies," said Mattie as they reached a white NOPD Crown Victoria with the blue POLICE slash along the side.

And so it was that with Catya and Maggie huddled together in the back seat going east with the blue lights flashing and the wah-wahs at full blast, Mattie hit the Port of New Orleans in under ten minutes.

"Holy shit, Mattie, are you all*owed* to do this?" said Catya as she and Maggie crept from the car.

But Mathias Dupree just smiled. "You see anybody trying to stop me?"

Catya grinned. *Still* the nice but naughty boy; she liked him for that.

And next they knew she and a pale Maggie were climbing aboard an NOPD Mississippi riverboat cruiser named "The New Normal."

~ * ~

After Spectral Sam's Kenworth House intervention, you might have expected Norman Gubbins not to honour his agreement with Mordy and Hazchem to a repeat meeting with Sir Keith Staniford but, partly because the elves had etched it into his memory as a must-do and partly because he reckoned he could now use it to his own advantage anyway, he did.

The occasion, held in Sir Keith's parliamentary office, began formally as might have been predicted, but ended frenetically, which could never have been foreseen given the normally unemotional natures of its two participants. His family aside, the only times Sir Keith displayed what you might think of as genuine passion were football related, either when scoring a goal for the Accies, for which leaping, ululating, and air punching were in order (joy), or after some travesty of justice handed down to Leeds United by an incompetent referee, which merited finger waggling and expletives (fury). Yes, his human rights ethics had been a lifelong passion too, but always a slow-burning one tempered by legal issues, as had been his association with socialist ideals. And as for Norman Gubbins, the only emotion *he* had ever experienced, apart from his peculiar experiences on Hampstead Heath, was the visceral desire for power he had now revivified full time after Spectral Sam's cajoling.

*Any*way, we're getting ahead of ourselves here. As noted (see above) the meeting began formally as might have been expected.

"Nice to meet you again, Mister Gubbins," said Sir Keith. "Good of you to come. Anything I can get you at all? Tea? Coffee?"

"No, I'm fine," said Norman, taking a seat across the desk behind which Sir Keith was sitting.

"Glad to hear it. So may I ask to what do I owe the pleasure of your company again? I've checked with my PA, Malcolm, and there doesn't appear to be a scheduled agenda."

Norman nodded his agreement.

"So?" said Sir Keith.

Which was when Norman embarked on the speech he had studiously rehearsed ahead of what he hoped would be a favourably life-changing moment. "I just felt I needed to set some matters straight with you after our last conversation," he lied, in much the same conciliatory manner he'd adopted on TV when accused of having broken the government's (*his*) own Covid lockdown travel restrictions by driving hundreds of miles up-country without anybody's knowledge or permission. "Would you be up for that?"

"If you feel it necessary," said Sir Keith.

And so it was that Norman launched into what verged on forty-five minutes of periphrastic hyperbole, which shall be omitted from this narrative for fear of inducing in the reader narcosis of the kind Sir Keith experienced while attempting to remain awake *and* encouragingly empathetic by occasionally nodding, smiling, and saying things like "mmm," "yes," and "I see" while simultaneously struggling to identify the subtext of so much increasingly emotional linguistic vacuity. Playing the psychotherapist in other words.

"Care to get to the point, old chap?" he struggled to stop himself saying at least thirteen times during Norman's disquisition. Sir Keith was a lawyer after all, and legal language is based on denotation not connotation, accuracy not flimflam. But on and on and *on* Norman blethered, sounding increasingly like his ex-boss Bruno Junkett when struggling off-topic to answer one of Sir Keith's specific questions in the House of Commons.

"Not boring you, I hope," he managed to say four or five times during the initial circumlocutions as Sir Keith topped up his water glass or took an unnatural interest in his shoelaces.

"No, no, not at all," Sir Keith would say, springing back to attention with a "Good heavens" or an "Is that *so?*"

And off Norman would go again, alluding to mistakes, missteps, misspeaks, misunderstandings, and all sorts of other missed things, ranging from a misspent childhood through a misspent youth to a misspent adulthood—*all* of them illustrated with lengthy diversionary narratives, including the deleterious influences of his father, mother, siblings, various aunts, uncles, cousins, Eton tutors, and suchlike. All a cynical strategy to gain sympathy, of course, to have Staniford believe he was a pitiable, poor, naïve, ill-done-by creature, misunderstood in all his behaviours, political or otherwise, especially when it came to his dealings with (Spectral) Sam Bundy.

Which was when Sir Keith woke up and took an interest in the "conversation."

"And how do you feel about Bundy now?" he said.

"Ashamed I should've ever taken his advice," a thespianly hangdog Norman muttered.

"I can understand that," said Sir Keith, because he could. After all, how deranged would a person have to be to sympathize with the madman who had been banned from even Twitter and Facebook for having posted the idea that ahead of the election two of Klank's worst enemies should be decapitated and their heads be put on spiked poles outside the White House for public display? Which, as Klank slid to what looked like inevitable defeat to Jack Bailey in the ongoing election, was precisely what Spectral Sam—under the pseudonym of Pussy Galore—*had* done from whatever instrument of mass communication he'd been permitted in his Coney Island prison.

Norman Gubbins hung his head and shook it in mock wonder when apprised of this latest slice of Bundy insanity. "You see what I mean?" he said.

"Indeed I do," said Sir Keith, beginning to wonder what the subtext of this uncharacteristic display of humility and self-pity was, and switching from psychoanalytic to lawyerly modes. "And may one ask why exactly you are in my office to tell me all this? It is not exactly as if in the past we've been what one might think of as confidantes."

It was in the saying of this that in Sir Keith's canny brain a number of tumblers fell into place, prime amongst them the suspicion Gubbins might just be looking for a new job after the Downing Street fiasco. As a revamped populist adviser to the Labour Party in its run-up to the next election, for example, selling him the sob story to get it.

Which was spot on. That was exactly why Gubbins was currently in Sir Keith's office. With Bruno Junkett surely following Dougal Klank down the toilet after a Tory night of the long knives, what Norman now needed most was a whole new wagon to which to hitch himself. For skills like his, surely there would be a market, and who cared if it happened to be a socialist one? Ethics had never been Norman's strong suit.

"Well, you see, I was wondering," he began in a tone that further alerted Sir Keith to possible subterfuge. "If...."

"I could give you a job?" said Sir Keith, eyebrows raised.

Which flummoxed Norman, who was unused to having his strategies so smartly unpicked. "Nuh-no, wuh-well, puh-*possibly...*"

"And then have you shoot me in *my* bottom the same way you shot Junkett in his?"

This was the moment the situation switched from the more or less formal to the frenetic.

"Huh-how duh-*dare* yuh-you suggest thu-that I...?" Norman fulminated, all vestiges of theatrical meekness vanishing.

"You to wonder, me to know," said Sir Keith. "Just let us say I have evidence upon which I can rely and leave it at that, shall we? Now please either confirm or deny your intentions for this meeting. I am a busy man."

Norman clenched his fist and growled, which wasn't a good plan, given the manner in which Sir Keith had dealt with a Guinness bottle flung at him and punches thrown during their previous meeting.

"Now, now, Norman," he said. "Let's not get overexcited, shall we? And puh-*lease* do not attempt the cardiac arrest con you pulled on me the last time we met. I am not a man to be fooled twice."

Norman snarled and banged a fist on the table separating the two men. "Me neither."

"So I can see. In any event, I am sorry to say I shall not be requiring your services for two reasons. Reason one: I am a socialist, not a populist. And reason two: I wish to ensure that both of my buttocks remain in good working order."

Which was when Norman saw not just red but vermilion and, while spitting teeth, upended the desk separating the two men, leapt over the detritus, and launched a haymaker at Sir Keith's jaw.

Bad move, because Sir Keith merely deflected the punch with a forearm that caught Norman off-balance and sent him teetering sideways towards a heavy old-fashioned standard lamp whose dislodged shade fell with uncanny precision over his head.

"Aaaaghhh," he screamed muffledly, while Sir Keith buzzed Malcolm into the office, outlined to him what had occurred and sought his PA's opinion on the advisability of informing the police.

"No real damage done but..." he said as Malcolm surveyed the scene and frowned.

"Enough to call the cops," Malcolm replied. "The bloke's clearly a danger to himself and others."

"My thinking, too, but it's good to get a second opinion. Give them a bell then, would you? I'll keep him quiet until they turn up."

"No probs," said Malcolm, heading for the door but turning as he did so to punch air and inform his boss Klank was so far behind in the key rustbelt states it could be assumed he'd lost the entire election, which Jack Bailey was already claiming, although this was only early November and he would have to wait for the final Electoral College declaration on December 14th for the victory to be complete.

"Yesssss," said Sir Keith, also punching air while standing on one of Norman's twitching feet. "At least that's *one* piece of good news today."

Seventeen

You know how it is with narcissists, how they go apeshit if confronted by humiliation or failure. Well, such was the case with Dougal Klank on November 7th 2020 except magnified by a factor of n, hence his public refusal to admit defeat in the election and his promise of the sundry lawsuits he would file against the Democrats who, according to him, had wilfully stolen the polls with illegally tainted ballots, for example, those mailed by dead people, Asian and Mexican immigrants without proper papers, and bribed anti-Klank Mafiosi. Mind you, even Twitter was beginning to tire of these baseless tirades from a person teetering on the verge of no longer being considered a "newsworthy individual." Pretty soon it would be banishing Klank from its platform for his scurrilous behaviour in regard to not only the entire election process but specifically his victorious opponent Jack Bailey.

Nonetheless, Klank continued to rant, rage, and swear vengeance, to which end he selfied himself wafting a baseball bat, looking furious, and promising all hell would be let loose before he could be persuaded to hand over the keys to the White House. All of which was food and drink to the equally rattled hillbillies and rednecks up and down the ex-Confederate states who took to polishing their 4x4s, loading them up with AK-47s and suchlike, and heading for anywhere they could cause mayhem. The immediate future for the US democracy looked bleak and riven, which was precisely what bad loser Klank wanted over the couple of months until he was forced out onto Pennsylvania Avenue wearing only the emperor's new clothes. Such was Dougal Klank's public response to his loss, that of a baby fulminating against his toys being taken away because he'd been an intolerable little shit who needed to be taught a lesson.

The private Klank seen by no one except his wife Melanoma and daughter Uwanka—even then only briefly when they were forced to stand by his side for photo ops—was in much less bellicose shape. All on his ownsome behind *very* closed doors in an eerily empty White House practically bereft of Covid-positive staffers, he mewled, puked, and headbutted walls. The world's soon-to-be *ex*-Most Powerful Man even contemplated putting himself out of his own misery with a shotgun like Ernest Hemingway, but that aberration lasted only about two seconds, seeing as rule *numero uno* in the egomaniac's bible is: YOU ARE TOO WONDERFUL TO DIE, LET ALONE AT YOUR OWN HANDS. So on he battled, even when Twitter confirmed his status as a "non-newsworthy individual" and he was told he could soon expect the privileges of his account to cease. This was practically a mortal blow in itself, for irrelevance is something no dedicated narcissist can bear, especially one as addicted to self-adulation as Klank, whose entire existence was predicated on perpetually regenerated glorification and revenge against those who didn't lavish it on him in abundance. His tweet tool stripped from him, and unable to do anything to prevent it, he took a moody timeout to seek solace at his own Klank National Golf Club, but even there was unable to hit balls. Mind you, he'd never been much good at that anyway except in faux photos showing him hitting eagles, although in reality he mainly hit pigeons.

As in the case of his one-time mentor Sam Bundy (see above), you could almost feel sorry for the guy—*almost*. Only in the USA, nobody except the hillbillies and rednecks did. All thinking folks had voted Bailey, hence the expected election result. And the rest of the world pretty much agreed with them, glad as they were to see the back of the worst president America had ever had so the planet could be given a glimmer of hope in a Klankless future. Even the half-arsed sycophant and Klank clone, Bruno Junkett at 10 Downing Street, was obliged to offer a hypocritical thumbs-up to President-elect Bailey, although he dreaded his arrival on the world stage. The only person of significance not to share in the congratulations was Igor Ripyurpanzov in The Kremlin, but he was in no position to divulge his true feelings without admitting to fury at having lost the puppet Klank he had so carefully groomed over so many years and finally in 2016 helped win the White House with his (studiously disowned) Internet meddling.

~ * ~

In his creek off the mighty Mississippi, Silas Baudoin, Catya Rampersad, Maggie McKenzie, Mattie Dupree and Rufus whooped, hollered and barked when they heard the news of Klank's impending removal from the White House and did a little dance—a rumba in a copse of swamp maples on the fringes of the forest.

Back in the cabin later, exhausted but happy, the five of them collapsed onto the sparse furniture or on the pine wood floor and toasted each other with glasses of the Indian Wells cabernet Mattie had the foresight to bring along on The New Normal, just in case of a Bailey victory. Well, the four humans did. Rufus expressed his delight by gnawing noisily on one of his master's special vegan doggie bones and farting stentoriously.

"*Maannn*, this could be the happiest I've been since The Saints last won the Super Bowl, and that was a long time ago," Silas sighed, sprawled across one of the cabin's two tatty sofas. On the other sat Catya and Maggie holding hands, while Mattie took what might once have been an American rocker only it didn't rock any more.

"And what a time for an old fogey like me to be surrounded by all my favourite people," he added. "If there's a heaven, this is my idea of it. The blood runs faster. And faster still when I see the happiness on you gals' faces. Was a time when I struggled with same sex politics but learning never ends, huh?"

"Thanks for that, Uncle Silas, we love you, too," said Catya. "Not so, Maggie?"

"Forever," said Maggie. "One thing I am sure as hell sad about, though…"

"Is?" said Mattie, who knew his cousin worked in some capacity in Klank's White House but had no idea what her new partner did.

"That there's no chance now of me cutting off all of Klank's hair so he goes bald as Yul Brynner. I was sooo looking forward to doing that."

"We had it all planned," said Catya, throwing an arm around Maggie. "As the final solution. We talked about it, Uncle Silas, didn't we? In fact, it was *your* idea."

"It was?"

"Yeah, you remember?"

"Sweetheart, some parts of my memory are pretty much things of the past," said Silas. "But if you say it was true, then it must have been. Sure as hell would have been a good plan, though."

Mattie looked on wide-eyed. "Tell me more."

Catya checked the OK with a glance at Silas, who nodded and grinned. "The boy is only a policeman on the outside, honey. *Inside* he's a regular guy. Ain't that right, Mattie?"

"I'll tell no one, you got my word on that," said Mattie.

So Catya explained what she and Maggie had hoped to have in store for Dougal Klank, Mattie shaking his head and smiling as the logic registered.

"Great to have two gutsy gals like you in the family," he said when the explanation was over. "But who knows, Maggie, maybe you'll still get your chance. Way it sounds to me, the asshole ain't going noplace till he gets helicoptered outta the Shite House in chains, and he's gonna need a haircut before then, right?"

Maggie brightened. "True enough."

"And I wish you all the very best of luck with that. You'll keep me up to speed with it, Cat?"

"With great pleasure."

"Okay, just so you believe where my heart is, even though I'm a cop, how about we have a little fun music around here?" said Mattie, taking from his jacket a small tablet, booting up, and playing first a re-write of "New York, New York" portraying a happy city cleansed of Klanks, and then Roy Zimmerman's spoof version of "The Lion Sleeps Tonight."

Catya and Maggie fell about laughing while Silas picked up his battered old Gibson.

"The Tokens had the original version, right? Sometime back in the early sixties," he said.

"Spot on," said Mattie. "And you're the old dude with no memory."

Silas shrugged. "Don't apply to songs. Gimme another run-through, we'll see what lines we can remember, then mebbe we'll have us our own singsong. The chords are easy, and who knows, we could make up some of our own words."

"Raaf, *raaf*," said Rufus who had finished his vegan bone and liked it when Master played his guitar, especially on its ancient wind-up amplifier.

And so it was that all around the depths of Silas Baudoin's "mighty jungle" that night echoed sounds many of its resident creatures hadn't heard for a long while. And they liked them, howled and hollered and hooted their approval. Maybe it was only an Indian Wells cabernet-inspired fantasy, but it seemed to Catya, Maggie, and Mattie even the trees were sighing their relief from the threat of Dougal Klank having been finally expunged.

"Wooooeeeee," they seemed to be whispering, rustling their branches for backup.

~ * ~

In their Lake District hideaway, Mordecai and Hazchem were also pleased by the result but were aware too of Klank's refusal to concede defeat and the danger to American democracy that could be caused by the cronies he was tweeting and hiring to spread across the nation news of a battery of lawsuits claiming electoral foul play and fraud. That, and encouraging as much protest street violence as they could muster. Okay, it was fine for Mattie Dupree to believe Klank would eventually be helicoptered away in chains, but there were still the weeks meantime to be taken into account, in which he could employ a scorched earth policy to leave behind him. For one thing, he was still in possession of the nuclear football even if he didn't know how to use it. There were even stories he had discussed with the top military the possibility of bombing Iran's rumoured nuclear sites as an infernal swan song.

"So he can go out with a bang," said Mordy.

Hazchem nodded. "And take most of the rest of the world with him."

"Exactly. About which we are pretty much powerless to do anything. Just as we were over the Covid vaccines business, although the news is some are now in the process of being invented."

"We did do *some*thing then, though, didn't we, Mord? That time it was to bring two young women together."

"So we did and that seems to have worked out well," said Mordy, flicking around their Elf Information Highway screen to check on the current state of affairs up Silas Baudoin's lazy creek and closing in on an image of Catya and Maggie snuggled up together on a makeshift mattress with Rufus lying at their feet, grinning foolishly.

"Heart-warming," said Hazchem, morphing momentarily into a Rufus clone to get a feel for the dog's evident delight at being close to his new friends. "Poor guy's going to be sad when they leave."

Mordecai smiled. "Raaf, raaf," he said in the best imitation he could muster of Hazchem doggy-speak while scrolling back through earlier conversation in Silas's cabin.

"Tell you one thing we might manage, though, Hazza," he added, replaying the part in which Maggie bemoans no longer being able to shave Klank's head and Mattie says there might be the window of a chance before Klank finally got the boot from the White House.

"What's that?" said Hazchem, still in Rufus mode.

"Make Maggie's dream come true. World wars, deforestation and pandemics we might not have been able to prevent, although Oberon knows we did our best down the centuries, didn't we?"

"Indeed we did, Mordy."

"But some small powers we *do* still have."

"Raaf, raaf. Only they went a bit pear-shaped with Gubbins."

"Like many humans since the dawn of time, *that* one is beyond salvation and *tant pis* for him, as the French have it," said Mordy. "We did our best to suggest a new outlook on life but one can only guess that the Spectral Sam character was some boggart or other throwback determined to returned him to his previously cherished *self*, hence the latest foul-up with Keith Staniford."

Mordy spat the word "self" through clenched lips. "The damnation of the human species that causes them forever to look inwards not outwards. Me, me, me, mine, and then just a dash more me as they blindly pander to their own deluded belief in the ephemera of power at the expense of the wider realities that will eventually cripple them. Their history is crammed with the paradises of such fools, *vide* Klank's fate. But anyway, *any*way, all that aside," he added, calming down a little, "On the haircut issue, what is to stop us helping to arrange for Maggie McKenzie to rob Klank of his cherished locks and drive him even crazier than he already is before it's too late?"

"Nothing," said Hazchem. "Two birds with one stone, eh? No more hair, no more power or wriggle room for screwing up the planet."

"Right in one as always, Hazza. The critical conceit removed at the vital moment."

And so it was that plans were put in place to influence a mercifully Covid-free Hank O'Henry urgently to recall Catya and Maggie to the White House on the grounds they were amongst the tiny minority on the planet who sympathized with the soon-to-be-ex president's distress and wished to offer him their support for his attempts to reverse the election result by providing him with what was to be called "the haircut of all haircuts" entirely free of charge.

"Shouldn't be too hard to organize," said Mordy, as one of a sheep called Samantha ambled into the living room, said, "baa" and snuggled up to Hazchem, who morphed into collie mode for her greater comfort.

"Not at all," he said, "Easy-peasy. And then let's see how Klank feels about being shorn the way we would never allow our Samantha to be."

"Eh, Sam?" he added, ruffling the ewe's luxuriant coat which was never going to be sold to the highest bidder any more than the bodies of her current offspring, headed by Mike and Lucinda, were ever going to end up on dinner plates as either shank or cutlet of lamb.

"Baaaaa!" said Samantha, thanking her lucky stars for the day these two nice elves had taken possession of the Derwent Water hillside farm. Without them, who knew, she, her family and Ronnie the ram might already have found themselves either inhabiting humans' stomachs waiting to be disgorged as faeces or left shivering after sacrificing their wool to keep the bastards warm. At the very least, nice Mister Mordy and funny Mister Hazchem had brought a little order to the local ovine community and Samantha loved them for it.

~ * ~

Also inspired by Klank's downfall, down in London, Ramona and Rickie/Enrique/Henry Schmidt were wondering how further to capitalize on the smash-hit JawJaw bot that had broadcast to the world the true cause of Bruno Junkett's half-arsedness. Fine, so it had been a winner worldwide on social media and produced endless ribaldry and money, but you know how it is with folks who believe themselves to be in the fast lane, how they want to go faster still—in this case by pushing Junkett yet further towards the slippery slope Klank had slid down. Which was why Ramona was persuaded by Rickie/Enrique/Henry to contact JawJaw "amigo" Munich-based forty-five-year-old dissident *Alternative für Deutschland* supporter and faux psychiatrist Herr Professor Doktor Zigmat Frude (not his real name), to put together any argument he could manufacture explaining the linkage between damage to a person's sinistral buttock and the erosion of whichever of the brain's cortices he fancied. It was one thing for Junkett's physical half-arsedness to have performed as a witty metaphor for mental disability, but how much more potent and profitable would it be if backed by scientific evidence was Rickie's reasoning. *If* additionally, Frude could add into his diagnosis symptoms of long Covid of the kind presumably suffered by both Junkett and Klank—assuming the latter had truly *had* the disease—that would be a bonus. So, as the German speaker in the family, Ramona obliged.

In his Bogenhausen flatlet on the tatty outskirts of Munich, where he had been furiously locked down on Berlin's Covid orders for so long he could barely remember his birth name—Hermann Hofmann—Herr Professor Doktor Zigmat Frude was delighted by Ramona's email.

With no Oktoberfest or Xmas market to go to, no cheering news about European populism to hang on to, no woman (or man) in his life, Hermann was hanging onto existence pretty much by a thread. All the hopes he'd fostered about strong populist leaders ruling both Germany and the world now remained solely in the hands of Igor Ripyurpanzov in the Kremlin, given Klank was obviously terminally fucked and, according to reports in *Die Zeit*, Junkett didn't even understand *how* Gubbins' populist sloganeering had contributed to his power base, simply reckoning that being a popular buffoon was reason enough to enable him to run a country. Chuffed indeed, Hermann therefore was to receive Ramona Schmidt's message inviting his contribution to, and extension of, Jaw's Junkett backside story, *so* chuffed he replied immediately by Zoom, his most exciting lifeline to the outside world in these mind-bendingly lonely torpid Covid days.

"*Es wäre mir ein Vergnügen* (It would give me great pleasure) *Frau Schmidt*," he barked teutonically, champing at the bit to undertake the task. Which confused a feet-up-on-the-bed Rickie as he peered at the unfashionably unshaven straggly grey-haired person who'd suddenly Zoomed onto his iPad screen speaking a language clearly other than English.

"Mona, quick, quick, there's a nutter on the 'puter," he called to Ramona, who didn't like being called Mona because it sounded too much like Moaner and was in any case in the en-suite bathroom tub caked in Amazon Prime's most expensive foams, creams, and perfumes bought on the back of the Junkett's bottom bot.

"Oh, for fuck's *sake*, Rickie, can't you handle *any*thing on your own?" she retorted, yanking out the plug and thereby causing the water to drain noisily away.

Rickie turned the iPad screen to face an open wardrobe door in case Ramona were to walk naked into the bedroom and overexcite the crazy on the screen.

"*Frau Schmidt, ist etwas da los* (is something wrong there)?" asked a perplexed Hermann Hofmann/Herr Professor Doktor Zigmat Frude, confused at Rickie's yelling, the background liquid gurgling, and the sight of such wardrobe contents as frilly nightgowns. Worried in case he'd upset some domestic applecart.

"*Nichts, überhaupt nichts* (Nothing, nothing at all), *Herr Professor Doktor*," said Ramona, yanking the iPad from Rickie with one hand while holding a knee-length purple robe across her breasts with the other. Had she had a third hand, Ramona would have used it to flip Rickie/Enrique/Henry the finger. But she didn't, and in any case, Rickie was already preoccupied pretending to check tweets on his phone.

Just as well, Ramona pretty soon corrected Herr Professor Doktor Zigmat Frude/Hermann Hofmann's fears of domestic intrusion with calming German words and a lot of flattery. Otherwise his axial contribution to JawJaw might have bitten the dust even before inception. But Ramona knew her Germans and how to butter them up so, by the time she'd uttered soothing words and outlined to the Herr Professor Doktor his potential contribution to the balance of power in the UK and possibly even the EU, he was practically eating out of her hands. Hermann even contributed to the final deal with mangled fragments of the English language to which he should have devoted more study over the years, but consciously hadn't after his conversion to the notion that the lingo, particularly in its American version, was a tool of worldwide imperialistic domination.

"Zis Junkett I am sinking is ze ass's hole, *nicht wahr?*" he said, for example, with a half decent stab at a translation for the German *Arschloch.*

"Not so much 'hole' as semi-buttock, hence half-arsed," Ramona corrected pedantically. Which was difficult in German, but somehow she managed it. "Meaning he's about as useful as prime minister as a stuttering parrot with its head up its backside. And, by the way, as far as your proposed contribution is concerned, I would be enormously grateful if you would keep it down to a maximum of five hundred words with nothing too scientific or esoteric. What we need here is something punchy, easily understood, and memorable for the average Joe and Jane in the street. And it's fine with me in German. I'll do the translating. And any editing if necessary."

Hermann loved it. Perhaps *some* kind of new-world phoenix might still emerge from the embers of the once so successful sloganistic populist paranoia peddled by the likes of Bundy, Klank, Junkett *et al.* And if it meant him re-thinking his current affiliation to *Alternative für Deutschland*, so be it. So much for fake news, post-truth, and the *Gerede* (chatter) of the mindless who, now Hermann thought about it, had been the very ones to support Hitler and, so far as he understood it, the UK supporters of Brexit.

"Sanks, sanks, sanks zo much für ze tchob you give me," he said, in his best shot at English. Then he added in German how honoured he was to have been chosen for such an important mission and how he hoped it would help turn his life around. Maybe there was *still* the possibility of a better world after the insanity of Klank, and if his small contribution could help an iota in sending Junkett to a similar fate, he would feel his life had been led to some purpose after all. Also Frau Schmidt should not think of any payment for his work, which he would donate to this noble cause free of charge. She could expect its outcome just as soon as he had put the argument together.

With those words, he de-Zoomed, leaving Ramona on the one hand grateful for Frude's generous contribution but perplexed as to its reasoning. After all, she and Rickie were a whole lot more interested in profits for JawJaw than they were in airy-fairy ideas about changing the world.

"Rickie?" she said, keen to discuss the outcome of her Zoomathon with Prof Frude.

But Rickie/Enrique/Henry just sat up in bed, jammed the forefinger of his left hand across his lips, and with the other prodded meaningfully at the phone buds jammed into his ear, all of which translated as "Shhhh, I'm busy."

Eighteen

American democracy was threatened to its historically still fledgling roots during the days Dougal Klank ungraciously continued to not concede defeat to Jack Bailey, saying under no circumstances would he ever agree to such baloney and insisting to all "true Americans" it was *he*—the object of the "greatest witch hunt in American history"— who had won the rigged election and would continue in his attempts to get justice for his claims, so their next president would still be him.

Most irritated by this devious and divisive statement of course was Jack Bailey, who wanted nothing more than to get down to the business of preventing further millions of his fellow-countrymen and women from throwing in the towel to Covid-19. That was priority *numero uno*, although he had start-ups in mind for many other welfare projects and a significant American contribution to the global reduction in carbon emissions, something his predecessor had deemed beneath his dignity. He didn't allow the irritation to get him down, though.

"Honey, we play this my way by paying no attention. So far as I'm concerned, we won and I'm going to be president. Klank can shout all he wants, I've gone deaf," he told his wife Jenny, who throughout the campaign had taken time off from her daytime teaching job to accompany her husband all around the election trail.

She kissed him. "Way to go, Jack. It's the only thing I'd expect from you."

"Much appreciated as always, Jen. I love you, you know that, and it's been and still is a hard road for us both. But look...I'm a big boy now and any time you want to take a time-out and get back to your own work, you just shout."

"As and when, babe. You need me, I'm here."

"I am blessed and that's the truth," said Jack, whose anchor Jenny had been in respect of not only the turmoil of politics but also her husband's personal family tragedies.

Jenny drew a slow finger through his carefully coiffed snow-white hair. "And so are not only the American people, but folk all around the world with not just you as president but with the team you've been building."

Which was fair comment. While Klank's constantly changing team had comprised on average ninety-nine percent gung-ho white male yes-men with the odd woman thrown in as a gesture to his pussy-grabbing libidinous desires, already Bailey's early appointments to key posts included an equal balance of genders and ethnicities to mirror the new reflective governance of American society he was intent on building, amongst them the first black female vice president-elect in American history, Katy Paris. And this was not mere tokenism on Bailey's part, for each and every appointee was qualified to the eyeballs and could therefore be trusted to speak his or her own mind without reference to the president in the happy knowledge he and they would always be singing from the same hymn sheet. A matter of teamwork and trusted delegation, therefore, as opposed to Klank's paranoid fear of staff speaking out in disgust at whichever of the latest lunatic lines he had adopted on the spur of the moment, and would thus need firing.

~ * ~

In his multi-billion ruble Black Sea palace at Gelendzhik, Krasnodar Krai, Igor Ripyurpanzov choked on his postprandial vodka at the thought of the newly emergent Western liberal agenda he had so recently written off as past its sell-by date now resurfacing in the very country into which in 2016 he'd planted what he'd hoped would be a game changer in global power, such that two 'axes of evil' could finally meld into one.

~ * ~

In his newly refurbished 11 Downing Street apartment, Bruno Junkett wasn't best pleased either at witnessing his American election fears materialise and the impressive chappie who'd called him "my kinda guy" after the pair had met in Washington some years earlier so suddenly set to vanish from the world stage.

"Poor old Klankers," he muttered, while streaming Fox News broadcasts showing Klank looking outraged and vindictive.

Not that Bruno's empathy was genuine, of course. Nothing even remotely resembling altruism coursed through the Junkett veins. The sub-textual meaning of his muttering was "poor old *me*," seeing as he could no longer rely on the support of the leader of the world's greatest superpower for backup in his most audacious plans when it came to creating oligarchies. Okay, so *Gubb*ins' audacious plans, but he no longer had *that* turncoat's counsel to fall back on, either.

"Bugger, bugger, and bugger to bugger*ation*," said Bruno, pulling the plug on the D.C. streaming. "I bet the bastard Stanifart'll be smirking all over his ugly mug."

Which was a fair analysis of Sir Keith's response to the American news, only he wasn't smirking; he was smiling warmly as he watched Bailey shake the hand of each one of the new (mask-wearing) appointees behind him on stage before moving to the podium microphone to tell his countrymen and women what they could expect from his government and how it would reflect the original constitution, both figuratively and literally, of the whole nation.

"Big tasks ahead of us all from day one," he said. "Top of the list, Covid-19. But that will not deflect us from our other duties in the world, climate change and our contribution to its control as a prime consideration."

And so, to the delight of his US Zoom audience—and Sir Keith Staniford and his guest at the Chelsea flat, George Ballentine—Bailey ran down the list of things Klank had either ignored or poo-pooed for four years as fake news before promising to overturn them on his first day in office.

"Gimme five, bro," said George, raising a hand when the speech was over.

But, laughing, Sir Keith clued George up to the WHO-recommended elbow bump so they did that five times instead before Sir Keith took from his fridge a couple of chilly bottles of Guinness with which they toasted Jack Bailey, who'd been joined on stage by his wife Jenny.

"Genuine looking woman," said George. "Not one of those Klank sluts."

Bailey's virtual audience agreed. There were smiles on every face, including, thanks to Mattie Dupree's computer expertise, those of Silas Baudoin, Catya Rampersad, Maggie McKenzie and Mattie himself—as the new White House occupants held hands, kissed, then wished all Americans a happy but SAFE! Thanksgiving.

George shook his head in admiration. "Man, don't you just wish…"

"The same could happen on this little island," said Sir Keith.

"Sure. And that would be you and *your* good lady wife on that stage. How is Samantha, by the way?"

"She's good. I should see more of her and the kids, but the job doesn't always allow for it. Nor do I want the media knocking on the door with microphones in their hands."

George nodded. "See where you're coming from. But if one day you made it to Number Ten?"

Sir Keith raised an eyebrow. "That's a big *if*, George."

"Maybe, but I have a dream," said George, Martin Luther King Jr.-ishly. "And in it, Bruno sodding Junkett and his Government of brown-tongued cronies are axed by their own party and *you* and your lot take over."

Against all anti-Covid rules, Sir Keith gave his ex-teammate a macho hug just as he would have all those years ago when George had sent a twenty-yarder into the back of the net for the Accies.

"You're a friend, and from where I sit these days, that's gold dust," he said. "And while we're on the subject of cronies, got any further on tracking Gubbins down?"

"Sorry but no. Dead ends everywhere I looked."

"No theories at all?"

"None. I even checked out the Covid angle, in case I'd find him on some hospital list somewhere. Gubbins isn't a common name, after all, but how much use are Junkett's 'world-beating' test and trace gismos when you most need them?"

Sir Keith nodded ruefully. "None, as I have been telling him week after week in the Commons. And the Winnebago?"

"Gone from where he'd left it. Plus he must have wised up to *my* tracking methods, so no joy there either."

"Relatives?"

"All refused to speak to me. Up in Durham, they threatened to shoot me if I came near."

"And the cops' missing persons?"

"No record. Who knows, maybe he's sleeping rough or, maybe if he could blag his way through an airport, he's skipped the country and sold his soul to the highest bidder. One thing we *can* be sure of, though, he won't be welcome in Washington D.C. like he would have been by yesterday's news slimeball dictator. So blank sheet, bro. Sorry about that."

"Never mind," said Sir Keith. "You've done the best you could, lad. Want to catch up on the footie scores?"

Which was how he and George Ballentine spent the next hour. Mercifully Leeds United had won with a disputed VAR penalty and George's team Arsenal had thrashed Manchester City 4-0, which was reason enough for another round of chilly Guinness before Sir Keith reckoned it was time to call it a day and go home to Samantha and the kids. Where George called home, Sir Keith never asked, although he had the impression it was anywhere he hung his hat, which was pretty close to the mark.

On this night it would be with his "friend" Belinda who lived not far from the Hindu temple in Neasden. On one of the entrance paths to the temple, there was parked a Winnebago, but George didn't notice it as he drove past because he was too preoccupied thinking about Belinda with no clothes on.

~ * ~

German can be an infuriating language, particularly given its habit of shunting verbs off to the end of sentences so you don't know what they mean until you get to the full stop. A bit like reading a whodunit with a last chapter denouement. Plus it can be prolix and dense. How even little children know how to speak it is a mystery. Mind you, much the same can be said of *any* language we don't know, can't it? Think Japanese, for example. Or English, if you're Japanese.

*Any*way, like many academics, Hermann Hoffmann, aka Herr Professor Doktor Zigmat Frude, had built his career on introducing so much obfuscation into his rambling essays and single published tome as to render the entire opus practically incomprehensible. Which for many academics was an excellent way of ensuring invitations to lucrative international conferences to explain in simple language what it was they had really meant. Simplification of that order Hermann had, however, foresworn, arguing such "structuralist *reductio ad absurdums*" were anathema to him, hence producing even *more* abstract verbiage and intimations, concerning Freudianism for example, that in the end the whole shebang was a mystery, which was why it was so important not to reduce it to pedantry. And a nice little circuit he'd built for himself in Southern Germany, Austria, and Northern Italy, all of which as a bonus provided him with excellent opportunities to preaching his *Alternative für Deutschland* populism *and* have sex with young blonde women keen to plumb his depths after post-lecture libations. But those glory days were over, thanks mainly to increasing age and the *Gottverdammten* restrictions imposed on his movements by the bitch in Berlin just because of some super-hyped version of pneumonia.

From such a background in intellectual chicanery, you might have expected Ramona Schmidt to be disappointed with the Bruno Junkett buttock/brain conjunction email that pinged into her inbox only days after she'd requested it, but she wasn't. Far from it, she was delighted.

She had asked the professor for no more than five hundred words and, as the result of turning his brain inside out and back to front, Hermann had managed the task in only four hundred and ninety-four. He'd even come up with a catchy slogan for good measure. Okay, the whole thing was in German with its naughty end-of-sentence verbs, but Ramona was well versed in those and saw its translation as no problem.

Effectively, what Hermann had delivered was the somewhat obvious conclusion that all parts of the central nervous system from spinal cord to brain were in some way interconnected, and that it was therefore pretty obvious that the condition of the left buttock, albeit through a number of circuitous routes, was certain to influence the functioning of the cerebral cortices and vice versa. The witty twist, however, was the reference to Ezekiel 37:1-14, which had given birth to the old American gospel song "Dem Dry Bones." Given his dodgy command of English, particularly in its American version, Hermann hadn't bothered listening to the song, but he knew his Old Testament all right and reckoned the reference might be just up Ramona's street for JawJaw. Which once she'd listened to The Delta Rhythm Boys' version, it surely was. If the toe bone, via a whole load of other bones, could end up being connected to the head bone, then Frude was right in assuming knackered left-buttock nerves could lead to knackered brain functions. Hence his slogan, which Ramona translated as "From Arse to Brain and Back Again," FABBA, when acronymized.

"What d'you reckon?" she asked Rickie/Enrique/Henry after she'd pitched her proposal of a brand-new JawJaw post containing four items:

1) A photo of Junkett looking gormless, which wouldn't be hard to find because that's how he always looked.

2) A rerun of the half-arsed story.

3) The "FABBA" acronym with an appropriate explanation.

4) A background track of The Delta Rhythm Boy's "Dem Dry Bones."

"Fantastic, super fan-fucking-*tastic*," said Rickie/Enrique/ Henry. "And where d'you get all this from?"

"Remember the nutter on the 'puter? The one I tried to tell you about only you were busy pretending to be busy?"

"Oh, *that* nutter?"

"The same."

"Wow," said Rickie/etc. noncommittally.

"So do we go with it?"

"We sure as hell do."

Nineteen

Hank O'Henry was never sure what inspired him to come up with the idea of offering Dougal Klank the "haircut of all haircuts" to help him in his campaign to avoid becoming a footnote in history. Sure, Catya's and Maggie's desires to shear the creep had been planted in his mind back in what seemed like some other lifetime and then been delayed by the prevailing circumstances, but here it was again, sitting up and begging to be addressed. But then Hank couldn't have known he had been the object of two elves' decision to bring to its conclusion Maggie McKenzie's long held desire on behalf of all the women Klank had groped or raped to administer her version of justice. Anyway, wherever the idea had come from, he called Catya down in New Orleans where she and Maggie were enjoying an extended post-election celebration holiday with Uncle Silas, although Mattie had gone back to town, his job, and his family.

"Hank? So great hearing from you," said Catya, on the new and perfectly clear line Mattie had set up for his uncle. "How's it going up there? The asshole gone yet?"

"Nope, he's still mooching around looking vicious and self-pitying."

"Both at the same time?"

"Yeah. It's hard trick to pull, but he's doing it. That's why I'm calling."

"Huh?"

"Because it just occurred to me now would be a good time for Maggie's Klank haircut if she's still up for it. I could tell him there's a gal out there who's sorry for him, who believes he *did* win the election and wants to give him a little good luck present to help him on his way to a better future, like winning the White House back in twenty-twenty-four, for example. Either him or one of his brood."

"Wowee, Hank, one helluva plan. Where d'you get it from?"

"I surely don't know. It just came to me now could be the time to strike while the iron was in the fire."

"I'm gonna pass you over to Maggie, scc how she feels about it."

Hurried whispering down the line while Hank waited, but then Maggie came on loud and clear.

"You're damn right I'd do it," she told Hank. "Call me Miss Merciless, but I'd kick that asshole in the nuts if he was hooked up to a ventilator in his death throes with the Covid he never had."

Hank raised an eyebrow, but lowered it quickly once Maggie explained her views on misogyny in general and rape in particular.

"Yeah, you're right," he agreed, "And once he's out of the Shite House, he's gonna be facing all kinds of ladies' lawsuits for just those crimes."

"Which I hope he loses and cost him a fortune. Meanwhile, lemme at him on the ladies' behalf," said Maggie. "I'm passing you back to Catya to make the arrangements. She's a Shite House insider, right?"

"Right."

"So you guys get it organised while I sharpen my scissors and set my clippers to *numero zero* super shave. You sure you don't want me to stab him in the head while I'm at it?"

"No, *no*, the haircut will do it," said Hank. "We don't want you up for murder one. Just take away his hair and you *are* practically killing the guy."

Maggie nodded reasonably. "Yeah, I guess you're right. Oookay then, here comes Catya back again."

"Hank, you deserve a Congressional medal," she said.

"Best not to leave it too long, though," said Hank.

"No worries. We'll be with you in two days. Just a question of hitching a ride into the city on Uncle Silas's nephew's cop-boat and then hitting the airport. Meantime, you take care and stay safe."

"Same back to you. Call me when you're in town and I'll get it all set up," said Hank before cutting the call.

When Catya and Maggie told Uncle Silas the plan he had once dreamt up was about to come to fruition, he slapped his thighs, grabbed his guitar and, to the tune of Elvis's "Hound Dog," ad-libbed his own version. The first verse was:

"You ain't nothing but an ex-prez,
Moanin' it weren't fair.
You ain't nothing but an ex-prez,
Moanin' it weren't fair.
Whole lot worse you gonna be feelin'
When you ain't got no hair."

In seconds Catya and Maggie were on their feet dancing the jive, while Rufus cantered around them wiggling his bottom in what he considered a rock 'n' roll manner.

~ * ~

George Ballentine had difficulty finding his bearings the morning—okay practically afternoon—following the night's exertions with Belinda. All he knew was he was lying alone naked and sweaty on a king size bed whose red-and-white-striped duvet appeared to have flown away onto the floor. On the sheets remained the wondrous aromas of Belinda, but as with some difficulty he raised himself on an elbow and periscoped around him, the woman in question was nowhere to be seen.

"Lindie-*loo-oo*, where're you-*oo-oo*?" he trilled hopefully but to no avail.

So, shaking his head, he took to gathering together his clothes, which lay where he had stripped out of them in various corners of the tiny bedroom and took to putting them back on. This task, and a quick face splash in the shower room, occupied the better part of fifteen minutes, after which he tried the Lindie-loo call again and this time it was answered by the front door of the flat closing and Belinda shouting she was ho-*ooo*-me.

"Wondered where you'd got to," said George, peering down the stairs at the red track-suited woman currently busy with her warming-down exercises.

"Running," she said. "Don't you remember from the last time you came calling?"

Abashed, George didn't. But to cover up said, "Yes, of course, silly me. How many miles today?"

"Just the five like usual. I'd have asked you to join me only you were looking too shagged out, and anyway you were sleeping. Plus I didn't reckon you'd brought the right kit with you."

Which was true enough. The only clothes George had come with were the ones he was standing in.

"Sorry," he said. "How about I fix breakfast while you take a shower?"

"Now *there*'s an offer I can't refuse," said Belinda, stripping out of her running gear and heading upstairs covered in only the slight film of sweat over her nakedness.

Understandably Pete—that was what George called his penis—reacted inappropriately and required a crotch-covering hand to divert attention from his tumescence. But Belinda just smiled.

"You want an*other* go?" she said.

"You betcha," said Pete, speaking on behalf of his master, who grinned foolishly.

"You boys, huh?" said Belinda, who wasn't a whore, in case you were wondering. To set matters straight, Belinda was a lawyer of Jamaican descent who, with George's constant support, was a key member of the local post-George Floyd murder Black Lives Matter movement, which was also offered free legal advice by Sir Keith Staniford.

"Sorry," said Pete's master.

"Don't be, babe. You want it before the shower or after?"

George didn't answer that, just took her hand and led her back to the bedroom.

Pete was pleased with the decision.

It was two hours and twenty minutes later, after even more sex and breakfast, that Belinda reckoned a stroll through the neighbourhood might do them both some good. So it was that, holding hands and talking racial politics, the pair emerged onto the streets of Neasden for a little fresh air.

"You ever checked out our Hindu temple?" Belinda asked.

"I drove past it on the way to yours but no I've never..." George was saying, until from nowhere the image of the parked Winnebago flashed across his mind. It could have been any *other* Winnebago than Norman Gubbins', of course, but how many such vehicles did a person see around London on an average day?

"The BAPS Shri Swaminarayan Mandir it's called," Belinda was saying. "Supposed to be the first Hindu temple in Europe. Hand built with the purest materials. A great place to sort out your worries and get a little peace."

"And can just anybody go in?"

"Of course."

"Mmm."

"What's all this about, George? Some worries *you*'ve got?"

"Not me, but maybe—just *may*be—a guy I've been trying to track down for Sir Keith. Ever heard of Norman Gubbins?"

"*That* bastard, sure I have. How much I'd like to throttle him I can't tell you. But what does he have to do with a Hindu temple?"

Which was when George explained about Gubbins' recent history with Sir Keith and how he drove a Winnebago like the one he suddenly remembered had been parked on an entrance road to the temple.

"And you think it could be his?"

"It's possible. Don't have my tracking gear with me right now, so there's no way I can be sure, but..."

"What, and he's hiding out with Hindus?"

"Humour me, Lindie."

"I'll do better than that, babe. D'you have a picture of the son of a bitch on your phone?"

"Sure."

"So hold my hand and I'll take you there. Let's see if we can find a swami who can help us out."

~ *~

It was unfortunate timing for Bruno Junkett that JawJaw's Herr Professor Doktor Zigmat Frude's "half-arsed" thesis with its catchy FABBA slogan and Delta Rhythm Boys back track should have appeared just as the PM was doing his Churchillian best to present himself as the saviour of the nation by buying up trillions of vials of a super-vaccine to keep "our feet on the neck of the beast" over the Xmas spendathon. Fair enough, he didn't claim the bug would be gone forever, but as long as enough old folk and key NHS workers were about to get jabbed, in Bruno's curious logic that somehow meant the rest of the population could shop till they dropped.

"Going to be epso*lute*ly super. Just a little pinprick and hey, presto! all shall be well and all manner of things shall be well," he prated. "It also means we can keep the shops open at Crimbo so you can all go out and spend yourselves silly. *And* we'll lift restrictions for four days so you and your family can get together in the festive season." Yet another of Bruno's "booster" speeches to show what a good chap he was. A pity the relaxation backfired and resulted in several thousand more Covid deaths by early 2021, but ignoring scientific warnings as to this possible outcome and, keen as always to switch the narrative to his benefit, on and on Bruno prattled.

"And who was the first to achieve this brilliant vaccine result? We the English, that's who," he boasted, citing Oxford's AstraZenica and evidently having forgotten or repressed the fact there were other equally effective products on the market. Like Pfizer, invented by a pair of Turkish scientists before being developed in Germany and the US.

Such chauvinistic inaccuracies were quickly echoed by the dopiest of Bruno's junior ministers, such as failed Education Secretary Gary Walliams, who went about saying things like England had the best scientists, the best health care system, the best track record for vaccines, the best *people*, the best bananas, the happiest rabbits, so we should all be jolly proud of ourselves. Which counter-productively pissed off the Americans, the Turks, the Germans and the rest of Europe at the precise moment the UK Brexit negotiators were struggling to do any kind of a deal with the European Union to maintain trade while keeping alive the sacred myth of sovereignty. To which cesspit of silliness Health Secretary Mike Peacock, wiping *faux* tears from his eyes, blithely added it was precisely *because* Brexit had freed the UK from the double-dealing Europeans that we had been able to steal several marches on the rest of the planet and come out top (vaccine) nation, which was where we'd belonged since 1066.

Mind you, despite all this fatuous hyperbole, there were plenty of canny folk around the British Isles—and not only the dyed-in-the-wool anti-vaxxers—who weren't automatically buying into miracle jab hype. Not giving a monkey's whether Brits were best, they remained suspicious of the speed at which the vaccine had been developed, trialled, and approved. Okay, so this was some form of new RNA super science, but there were still questions to be answered. Like, how long would immunity last? Like, what were its possible side effects? Like, as some scientists were suggesting, it might still be possible for a jabbed person to remain a carrier through Covid beasties living up his or her nose? Like, what if Covid variants developed? Could it in combination with them then become as deadly as the original bug against which it was supposed to provide immunity? And, of course, the social media were going crazy with conspiracy theories, one of which suggested what the jab really contained was a Deep State/QAnon microchip designed to penetrate people's DNA and make them buy into Dougal Klank's claims he never lost the election and to hunt down and kill anyone suggesting he had. The events of 2020 had bred many, many devious minds.

All of these objections, however, Bruno Junkett side-stepped or fiercely denied when pressed by "fake news" journos. Along he barrelled, blindly blathering about putting the *GRRREAT* back into the Britain of which he, like Churchill before him, was a paragon. At least, like Basil Fawlty in *Fawlty Towers*, he took the precaution not to mention WW2, but the sub-textual implications were as clear, namely what Britain always most needed was an enemy to be seen to defeat. Currently it was Covid, but now we had the best of British vaccine, we would crush that, too, just the way we had Hitler.

Not the time, when Bruno reckoned things were going so swimmingly, for the sudden repeat onto every global social media platform of JawJaw's "half-arsed" story, this time enhanced by its top-notch German scientist's analysis—*analysis*—of the manner in which damage to a person's left buttock could have severe repercussions on that person's capacity to think coherently as the result of concomitant impairment to the brain. Then there was that damned Negro spiritual tune to go with it *and* the sort of slogan of which the traitor Gubbins would have been proud: "From Arse to Brain and Back Again" or FABBA for short.

Within hours of its release, the whole world, pissed off as it was with Junkett's boasted AstraZenica success, was singing along to The Delta Rhythm Boy's "Dem Dry Bones."

In Washington D.C., even the normally taciturn Jack Bailey couldn't resist a nod and a smile. "Guy had it coming," he muttered to himself. "You ask for trouble, trouble is what you get. Ask Klank about it."

In Moscow, Igor Ripyurpanzov obviously required a translation of the text and the song, but was less than amused when it was provided. First the American stooge Klank voted down the toilet by a supposedly dormant damned democracy, now the Brit puppet Junkett being made a fool of. What, Igor wondered, was the world coming to if even the best laid plans of top notch dictators were to be torpedoed by algorithms even more powerful than their own. "*Chert voz'mi* (fuckin' hell)," he said.

In Brussels, the president of the European Commission, Yolande de la Zouche, smacked her cheeks with both hands before releasing one of them to throw her phone at a wall after asking a passing gofer why the hell he was grinning and dancing the way he was and him explaining by showing her the new JawJaw release.

"*Merde, espèce de connard*" ("Shit, you son of a bitch") said Yolande in a moment of understandable Gallic passion.

What, after all, had been the point of the very, *very* last ditch telephonic and over-dinner attempts to persuade Junkett to ditch the UK sovereignty bollocks that got him elected prime minister in the first place, and consider instead the general European trading benefits post-Brexit if the guy had now been irrefutably diagnosed by a respected German psychiatrist as, for medical reasons, only being capable of thinking through his arse and even then only one half of it?

Not that Yolande was entirely surprised...she'd always suspected a malfunction in the Junkett brain, but had until now attributed it only to a narcissistic solipsism like Klank's, resulting from appallingly wealthy yet dysfunctional childhoods. Okay, the JawJaw piece might be just one more example of over-imaginative bullshit, but somehow it rang true. And yet here the dickhead now was shooting his mouth off on the crest of some vaccine success over the future of *Grrr*eat Britain.

"*Plus jamais*" ("Never again"), said Yolande.

Such were the views of just a few world leaders. Obviously, there were many more, but just let us say they were all in a similar vein. Meanwhile "Junkers," as he was now thinking to re-brand himself, waved two fingers at the JawJaw piece and media reports of its impact, drew a line under the whole nefarious episode, and hitched himself yet closer to the glorious panacea of the Oxford AstraZenica band wagon. Nothing half-arsed about *that*, he reckoned.

Twenty

Before going any further towards the Neasden Hindu Temple, George checked to see if the suspect Winnebago was still where he had last glimpsed it, which it wasn't.

"Mmm," he said. "Maybe I made a mistake and it wasn't his. Or maybe it *was* but he'd just dossed down in it overnight before moving on."

"Or perhaps he's been offered a parking spot somewhere out of sight," said Belinda. "This is a big place."

George had to agree as the pair came closer to the impressive white structure rising skywards. "When was it built?"

"Dunno, but it was opened in 1995."

"Wow, so recent."

"Yeah. Anyway, there's only one way to find out if your boy's here. By knocking on the front door, right?"

"Right. It all seems pretty quiet, though," said George as the pair paused to don their face masks.

Belinda raised an eyebrow. "It's a temple, not a bingo hall."

"True enough," said George, who wasn't a regular temple-goer.

"There was talk of a temporary closure in one of the Covid lockdowns or tiers or whatever they're called, but maybe like other churches that was just for public worship. You can bet your life this crew wouldn't turn away the needy."

Which proved to be the case when George and Belinda came across a saffron-robed, grey-bearded swami who was busying himself sweeping away dust and debris from the entrance stairway and, looking up from his labours, calmly donned his face mask as the pair approached.

"Always a job to do," he explained. "What makes life worth living, isn't it?"

George smiled, joined his palms across his heart, and bowed his head slightly in what he hoped was a fair replica of a respectful Hindu greeting, and Belinda followed suit. The swami set aside his broom and returned the gestures before asking how he might be of assistance to the lady and the gentleman today.

Before answering, George took a moment to register the calm that seemed to emanate from the man's pores. Every movement a slow one, as if the world around here operated at a different pace from the mayhem outside. Okay, it might have been a cliché-ridden response, but there was no denying the inner peace George felt. The same appeared to be true for Belinda, who normally operated at Mach Two, but whose body, when George took her floppy hand, had decelerated to a rate equivalent to that of a sunbathing heron.

Watching on, the swami nodded appreciatively. "If you are troubled, you have come to the right place. May I offer you a cup of tea?"

"That would be lovely," said Belinda.

"And your names, may one ask?"

George made the introductions.

"And I am Paresh," said the swami. "Paresh Singh, one of the teachers around here. Please to follow."

Once inside the temple, George and Belinda were ushered into a small room simply appointed in shades of gold, red and pink.

"Please to sit," said Paresh, gesturing with an opened palm at a three-seater sofa with cushions and an antimacassar in similar shades.

"So great to see such colours," said Belinda, sitting and stroking the upholstery. "All you ever see in English houses is beige and white."

Paresh nodded and smiled noncommittally. "Colour matters to the soul," he said, plugging in an elaborate three-layered golden samovar. "In a moment, the tea will be made and, if you wish, we can talk. Not about coronavirus or Brexit, if this is acceptable to you. Of these subjects a person has the nose full, as the Germans say. But if there are emotional troubles of concern, then I am at your disposal."

George nodded grateful understanding.

Belinda sighed and lay back against the sofa, which was a blessed relief after a hard day's night of sex and running.

It was after swami Paresh had poured the milk-and-sugarless tea into tiny silver cups on a sliver salver, added a plate of tukdi (spicy Indian biscuits) and placed the ensemble before his guests asking them to help themselves, that George, almost reluctantly, confessed the reason for their visit.

"We have no particular troubles, apart from the dreaded Covid and Brexit you wisely didn't want us to talk about anyway. No, it's somebody else's possible problems that concern us."

Paresh frowned slightly." Of *other* people's problems I cannot speak. We have our rules, confidential top of the list, isn't it?

"Of course. All I really need to know is if you've ever seen this man?" said George, showing Paresh Gubbins' picture on his phone.

"Why you are asking?"

"It's just that I need to speak to him and I thought I saw his Winnebago parked near here last night."

Paresh nodded. "The big car for sleeping?"

Pleased at the possible recognition, George confirmed such was the case, while Paresh continued to stare at the picture, the normally benign smile morphing into the faintest traces of a scowl.

"You've seen him before," whispered Belinda.

Which was when Paresh broke his confidentiality code and, as if wishing to cleanse his soul of the memory, said, "Yes, this is a very bad man," before outlining the purpose of Norman's brief visit the previous night.

"He seems upset, so I offer him my time and my blessings," he continued. "At first he is thankful and I bring him inside but…"

Paresh lowered his head and raked his brow with tense fingers.

"But?" said Belinda, extending an arm towards the old man.

"Then he goes crazy and throws things about. Valuable things. Not *money* valuable, spiritual valuable. I say 'Stop, stop' but he goes on, saying we gotta go back to India with our filthy religion. So I call two of my brothers for help. But, Miss Belinda, we are non-violent people and we have no means to…"

"Kick his arse out into the street," said George, whom it would have given the greatest pleasure to do just that and more.

Paresh semi-smiled. "Exactly. But then his phone rings and he says, 'Only if you give me my gong, you slimy…' I cannot say the next word he used, and before we know it, he and his Vinniebago are gone. This is my story…it is all I know."

"I am so sorry. You did not deserve such rudeness. Your information is useful for me, though. Is it allowed in your philosophy for me to give you a hug?" said George.

"Yes, but in these pandemical days?"

"Sure, okay, point taken. Just let's *think* hugging. How about that?"

Paresh smiled. "Think-hugging I can do. For the Hindu, reflection is the stuff of life."

"I wish it were for more of our people," said Belinda.

"We help where we can," said Paresh. "But there are obstacles. Emptying the mind can be a hard task."

It was to a greater understanding of the swami's philosophy that the following hour and a half was devoted, but once the tea and tukdi were all gone and the conversation concluded, George and Belinda thanked Paresh profusely and, reluctantly almost, took their leave.

"Some guy," said George as they unhooked their masks and made their way back to the flat. "Maybe one day I'll go back for more."

Belinda raised her eyebrows, grinned and rubbed a thigh. "By all means. But keep this in your emptied mind, sweetheart—swamis don't get a whole lot of sex. By the way, who d'you reckon Gubbins was calling a slimy so-and-so?"

"Bastard? Arsehole? Fuckwit? Prick? The Prime Minister of the Disunited Kingdom would be my best bet."

"Junkett?"

"The same. Gubbins used to be his main brain feed, but then for whatever reason there was some kind of a bust-up and he either ran away or was given the boot. Nobody knows which."

"Paresh said something about a gong."

George nodded. "Well spotted. That's right, he did."

"And he wouldn't go back without it."

"Mmm, I'll pass that along to Sir Keith."

"And what's your interest in the bloke anyway?"

So, as they strolled towards the Neasden Recreation Ground on the southern bank of the Brent Reservoir, George told Belinda everything he knew. Which was unusual for George, who normally revealed nothing of his daytime activities to the ladies in whose houses he sometimes hung his hat. But something previously intangible about Belinda had started seeping into his mind, making him wonder if this was what love was all about. It was also true this lady was, after all, a key member of the Black Lives Matter movement, so her knowing more about George's daytime job and recent work with Keith Staniford could hardly lead to leaks or disasters.

Belinda smiled. "You are a man of many talents."

"I wouldn't go *that* far, darling," said George, taking her hand and squeezing. "But thanks anyway."

"My pleasure...darling."

There isn't sufficient space in this account for time to be devoted to the developing George/Belinda romance, which could be the substance of a whole new story. But let's just say it happened, okay? And in coming years was to produce four children: two boys and two girls. So that was one good thing to come from the crazy twenty-twenty Covid times.

~ * ~

In America, newly face-lifted Dougal Klank was spending the last days of his lame-duck presidency raging around the country protesting his election victory at rallies in state after state despite being told to "take a hike, loser" by the legal eagles in all of them. Even the Senate had binned with contempt the latest of his claims to remain in the White House, effectively telling him to shut his (fake) face, and only the previous day the electoral college votes giving Bailey victory had been confirmed. Mind you, these lying, cheating, disclaiming, and distorting days on the road had so far netted Klank around $350m to put towards his pension pot and time was running out to turn that into his target of $400m before Jack Bailey got sworn in. Maybe he could get back his old TV role, maybe anything, but he sure as shit was going to need a shedload of dollars to defend all the lawsuits coming his way once the presidency shield had been lifted. To help pass the time and take his mind off such irksome prospects, he took to pardoning all his ex-chums, including Sam Bundy, accused of heinous crimes against both persons and the state, while turning a deaf ear to clemency appeals from those across the nation on death row for whom he overtly encouraged the firing squad option. Nobody around the White House for him to fire any longer, nobody around to take his picture while he held aloft signed diktats either, so still in his trademark blue suit with his red tie, he sat behind his desk impressing nobody. Peering through a window, Hank O'Henry reckoned this might be just the moment to suggest the haircut of all haircuts. Catya Rampersad and Maggie McKenzie were in the building on red alert; the stage was set, so why not give it a go?

Entering the Square Office after the requisite three scratches on the door much in the manner of a courtier at Louis XIV's Versailles palace, Henry kicked off with, "Anything I can get you today, Mister President?"

Klank still insisted on being called Mister President even when technically he wasn't. Sometimes, like today, he had to be called Mister President four times before he would answer. It wasn't until Hank was gearing up to embark on number five that the bloated and blotched skin-stretched face looked up.

"Yeah, you sure can," it said. "You can get me recounts in Pennsylvania, Wisconsin, Georgia, Texas, Wyoming, Massachusetts, Alaska, Oklahoma, California, Florida and um…" it continued before running out of states' names. Klank's hold on geography, even of his own country, had never been great. "All the other goddam rigged places where *I* got all the votes but the other guy got elected."

Hank bowed his head in sympathy. "The greatest miscarriage of justice in American, possibly *world*, history, Mister President."

"You can say *that* again, Hunk."

So Hank did, while Klank scowled and took to tearing pages from his leather-bound "Presidential Proclamations" book and tossing them in the air.

"When you think of all the great things I *did* for this country."

Hank couldn't think of any great things but clearly this was the wrong moment to be contentious.

"With *me* at the helm, it's been a freaking paradise."

It was with some difficulty that Hank choked back the urge to remind/tell "Mister President" of the sixteen million of his fellow citizens currently suffering with Covid-19 and the three hundred thousand who had died while he hadn't lifted a finger to help them, asserting the bug would just "go away" of its own accord.

"Sump'n wrong with your throat, Hunk?"

How Hank O'Henry wanted to punch this flabby freak in the face, up-end the chair he was sitting on, then kick him in the nuts till they dropped off. *If* he had nuts, that was. It was with an act of thespianly heroic dimensions that he managed to assure Klank there was nothing wrong with his throat, but he did have a suggestion that might appeal as a gesture of solidarity and empathy with Mister President's dreadful predicament.

"So hit me, Hunk."

Hank was balling a fist behind his back as, on behalf of "two gals of his acquaintance" who were the solidest of solid Klank supporters he offered their humble gift of a haircut to rival *any* ever experienced by the leader of *any* country in recorded history.

"They pretty with cute asses and big boobs?" said Klank.

Hank assured him they were.

"Ookay, so I'm good with the plan. I sure need a little light relief around here," said the soon-to-be ex-president, who had just got off the phone after an hour-long tussle with Georgia's Secretary of State, demanding he find the 11,780 votes he reckoned he needed to prove for once and for all he had won the state and therefore the entire election. Once that was achieved, what Klank had in mind was some sort of far-right insurrection across the USA demanding justice be done, if necessary with military intervention.

"Plus I could use a cola and a burger."

"Coming right up," said Hank, taking his leave and giving a Zoomed thumbs up to Catya and Maggie.

"Got all your kit primed and ready to go?" he asked Maggie.

"Sure I do."

"Including the hair root death treatment?"

"Including that."

"And how'd you figure we go, with your hypodermic or my sleep-spiked cola?"

It was Catya who came on the line to decide that question in favour of the spiked cola. "Second thoughts, it could be kinda difficult getting the hypo into his ass."

Hank nodded. "True enough. Okey dokey. See you soon as you're ready."

"You got it," said Maggie.

Twenty-one

Unlike the old days when he would swagger into 10 Downing Street through the front door, this time around Norman Gubbins slid into the building through a back door servants' entrance before making his way to Bruno Junkett's private office.

"You called," he said. "But don't think of this as some mercy visit. No gong, no sudden return to my substituting for the brain you haven't got, okay?"

Had he been a more sensitive soul, Norman might have noticed his once exuberant ex-boss looking doleful, depleted, and yes, doolally, even by comparison with the not-so-old days. Even the wicked glint in the eyes beneath their unnervingly slanting brows and toilet brush hairstyle had gone. But, not having a soul, let alone a sensitive one, Norman noticed none of these things. Okay, the fucker looked a bit shagged out, but that was the size of it, from Norman's perspective.

"Answer me or I'm out of here," he said, to which Bruno responded by blinking a bit then patting the chair beside him in his idea of welcome.

"Sit," said a prime minster battered on all sides by:

1) Domestic and worldwide ridicule after "Professor Frude's" JawJaw exposé about the linkage between physical and mental half-arsedness,

2) Accusations of serial incompetence, dithering, and yet again being "behind the curve" over arrangements for Xmas, especially given the appearance of the new super-spreader Covid variant. More dithering until advice from all the top scientists finally managed to persuade him the event was best cancelled altogether, as it should have been at least a week earlier before folk had made their Yuletide plans This was according to not only the top scientists, but also Sir Keith Staniford, many in Junkett's own Tory party and, alarmingly, most of the normally gung-ho right-wing press.

3) Criticism from the Europeans *and* the UK Brexiteers for being unable for once and for all to make up his mind whether he was going to sacrifice "sovereignty" over European fishing rights in British waters, thereby compounding the Covid and Brexit problems into a full-on national disaster.

In short, the gormless optimism Junkett had managed to preserve unchallenged for all these years was now in danger of being blown out of the water. Transparent had become his tried, tested, and now exposed technique of blethering a bit about whatever problem was on the table before disappearing and leaving the solution to someone else who could then be fired if it went wrong. This included *all* the numbskull members of his cabinet, many of whom were already considering resignation.

Gubbins had been different, though. Gubbins was streetwise, smart, and worth every penny of the fifty-grand pay rise he'd been given before getting all huffy and walking away just because he hadn't been made a knight of the bally realm. And now Bruno needed him more than ever.

"Sit, man," repeated the multi-conflicted and possibly soon-to-be ex-prime minister, patting at the chair beside him till his hand hurt.

But Norman didn't. Just took to strolling around the office looking ominous, while taking smartphone snaps of the PM.

"For God's sake, Gubbins," Junkett protested. "This is a *private* place, a sanctuary nobody can..."

"Shut it, Bruno. Now, unless you want me to release to the national and social media these pictures of you looking demented, thereby adding photographic evidence of the relationship between what's left of your arse and your brain, you will get on the phone right now to Missus Queen and register me for my knighthood in recognition of services rendered to the maintenance of Her sovereignty over such petty nations as France, Germany, Italy and others too numerous to mention as the result of my Brexit contribution."

There it was again, that magically empty abstract noun "sovereignty," which along with the highly regarded and equally vacuous "need for change" notion had been seminal keys to the 2016 EU "Leavers" 52/48% victory over the Remainers.

Bruno took to slapping his temples with both palms, which wasn't a great plan because Norman simply took more snaps.

"Nice head-slapping, PM," he said. "They'll sit well in the collection. Now how about you get on the blower to Missus Queen?"

"I kuh-kuh-*caaaan't,*" Bruno shrieked. "She wuh-won't tuh-talk to me anymore. She suh-says I luh-lied to her once over guh-getting huh-her permission to puh-prologue puh-Parliament for a bit to stop all the annoying backbiting. You remember that?"

Given it was he who had suggested it, Norman remembered the Parliament ruse only too well. If he'd had his way, the place would have been shut down altogether and forever. How was a person supposed to run a country with *that* bunch of nit-picking oiks arguing about every damn thing? What he didn't buy was the queen bollocks. On that subject, he nodded knowingly and said, "You're lying now too, you fat slug. Missus Queen *can't* tell her PM she won't talk to him."

"Yes, she bally well can. Prob'ly being egged on by the duke, who's always been jealous of my success," Bruno fumed.

Which was unwise, because the sudden switch to fume-mode caused him to writhe on his chair with the inevitable result of falling off it due to sudden left buttock deflation of the kind Rupert Splinsky had so cunningly inbuilt to respond to moments of personal distress.

"Just hold that pose right there," said Norman, looming over the fallen, moaning prime minister with his smartphone clickety-clicking. "This is going to look sooo good in the papers and on JawJaw."

Rolling with some effort onto his stomach, Junkett took to gnawing at Norman's ankles, which also wasn't wise because it gave Norman the excuse to kick him in the bollocks.

"Aaaaaaggghhh," said Bruno, curling up foetally and clutching his preciouses.

"Serves you right, you lying prat. And like I said, no gong for Gubbins, no more Gubbins making up what you think of as your mind for you," Norman was saying as the prime ministerial hot line took to flashing.

"I'll get that," said Norman, seeing as Bruno was in no position to get anything.

"Nuh-nuh-nuh-*NOOOOOOOOOOOOO*," croaked Bruno, but Norman, doing his well-practised Bruno Junkett impersonation in reply to Yolande de la Zouche's call, was already warming to the opportunity of giving her *his* views on the possibility of a last-minute Brussels trade deal on crucial matters such as fishing rights and their supervision. Not that he dwelt long on that subject, preferring to tell Yolande she had nice tits and he'd like to fuck her. No wonder the crucial Brexit talks stalled so suddenly and the following day's European and British newspapers were stuffed to the gills with stories of Junkett's serial philandering down the years.

All in all, this was *not* a good day at the office for Bruno Junkett, particularly in regard to the snaps Norman had taken of him looking even more gormless than usual. Once *they* were released to the traditional and social media—Ramona and Rickie were delighted with them—Junkett's poll ratings dipped to knocking on zero.

~ * ~

"You wonder how these Covid and Brexit catastrophes-in-waiting are going to play out if we leave them all to humans to sort out, don't you?" said Mordecai to Hazchem as the pair passed a FairyBac pipe back and forth in front of a log fire in their Lakeland farmhouse, having caught up with current affairs on their EIH (Elf Information Highway) screen.

"One does," said Hazchem, who on occasion adopted posh language just for the hell of it.

"Not so much in America," Mordy continued. "I like the Bailey bloke and the good things he's got on his agenda. Like joining back up with the Paris Climate Agreement and wanting serious connections with the Europeans once Klank's finally out of the picture."

"And about to get all his hair cut off," Hazchem reminded him. "*That* part we didn't leave to humans. Maggie will do the cutting but without that little chat with Hank O'Henry after we'd given him the idea…"

"She might not have."

"Exactly," Hazchem was saying as Samantha made her way into the room with Mike and Lucinda in tow and said, "Baaaaa," which translated as, "Make room for us in front of the fire, chaps."

Mordy and Hazchem re-arranged their chairs accordingly as the ewe and her lambs snuggled together, bleated a bit, and then fell happily silent.

"But now it's all set up, possibly happening as we speak," Hazchem continued. "You've seen the latest from the Shite House."

"I have and I can't wait to see Klank's face when he wakes up, stands up, and looks in the mirror. Munch's *The Scream* comes to mind, but will be small beer by comparison. You know the picture?"

"Sure I do. Me and Edvard talked it through before he hit the canvas with his brushes," said Hazchem, whose posh syntax also slipped from time to time.

"So no need to worry too much about America. But what in Oberon's name are we going to do about the country we call home? Okay, we elves are immune from dumb viruses, however much they mutate, but does one *really* want to go on residing in a country run by a self-serving maniac like Junkett and his bunch of shiny-faced, braindead toadies?"

"No, I'm ashamed to be a citizen," said Hazchem.

"Me too. Not that I've got any time for the creep Gubbins, either, especially after the personality re-think we offered him and he turned down. Okay, so now he's going for Junkett's jugular, but from concern for the welfare of the nation? Methinks not…instead from envy, spite, rancour and the same hubris that pumps through Junkett's veins.

We are locked, my old friend, in a country governed by lowlifes of the *low*est order."

It was around then that Samantha farted her agreement, thereby delaying proceedings while Mordy cleansed the air with super-elf deodoriser released from the index finger of his left hand.

"With the possible exception of the Keith Staniford guy," said Hazchem, reaching across to take the preferred FairyBac pipe and toking pleasurably. "Only he's not in government."

"Yet," said Mordy.

"You mean...?"

Mordy took to twining the ends of his long white beard around selected fingers. "I'm not sure *what* I mean. If what you're asking is should we start meddling in politics in ways we've always preferred not to unless absolutely necessary, then I take your point and the answer should be no."

"But?" said Hazchem tickling Mike's and Lucinda's toes and thereby causing paroxysms of pleasure as the lambs practised their roly-polies.

"And what if we were serving the general good? That was our rule down the centuries, was it not?"

Hazchem nodded and passed back the pipe. "True enough."

"Which we didn't need to do in the case of America," said Mordy, "because there was an election and the brave citizens did it for us. Okay, so we arrange for Klank to get his all his hair cut off because he deserves the final humiliation, but that's a side issue. In the UK there's no election on the cards for another four years, which is a long time to be stuck with jitterbug Junkett in charge. Unless, of course, there's a motion of no confidence."

"Which is?" asked Hazchem, whose familiarity with British parliamentary procedures was limited.

"A way of ditching a failing government. It needs the backing of a majority of MPs and, if it's passed, gives fourteen days for a different PM to take over, otherwise its general election time."

Hazchem shook his head. "Which is none of our business to organise."

"Quite. And even if it were, there's no guarantee of getting Staniford a new job. First of all, Junkett has an eighty-seat majority to rest on and all of them owe their seats to him having won them the last general election, so they're going to be *very* careful about no confidence votes. And even if they weren't and he got the boot, there are even worse than him in the party."

Hazchem rolled his eyes. "Worse than *Junkett?*"

"Afraid so. And you can bet your life they wouldn't be going for a general election to let the reds back in. Soooo…"

Mordy sighed.

"Not much of our "general good" in *that* scenario," said Hazchem, mussing Samantha's woolly coat, which caused her to stretch out her legs and say "baaaaaa" in satisfaction.

"None. I'm afraid we are stuck in this sad plagued island for the foreseeable, unless of course we did a bunk over to the US where matters are now more to our taste."

"And leave Samantha and her children to be shorn and eaten by cannibals? Mordy, *Mordy*, how could you even suggest…?"

Mordecai grinned and handed back the FairyBac pipe. "Exactly the response I'd expected from you, my old friend. Which is precisely why I have cherished your companionship across all of these years and have no intention now of seeing it challenged."

"Mercy bowcoop," said Hazchem, who occasionally fancied himself something of a Francophile.

"*Je t'en prie*," Mordy replied in a manner more likely to be understood by a French person.

Twenty-two

Norman Gubbins was furious when he learned of the last-minute Brexit deal that had been hammered out between the Brits and the Europeans even after his frank telephone conversation with Yolande de la Zouche and the posting on JawJaw of his snaps of Bruno looking even more bonkers than usual. Furious not so much with the deal itself but with Junkett's triumphalist crowing about how he had single-handedly preserved the nation's prized sovereignty and taken back control as promised in 2016. Not that he would ever read a word of the thousand-odd page document generated in Brussels, of course. That's what pointy-heads and lawyers were for, wasn't it? No, no, what Bruno would do was to swagger about doing his Winston Churchill number and very visibly putting the Great back into Britain.

"Sodding little twat," growled Norman, sprawled on a bunk at the back of his Winnebago. "Who was it who wrote the 2016 Brexit script for him? *Me!* Who was it who got the fart elected PM? *Me!* And who's getting all the credit for a Brexit deal he never wanted because what he really wanted was a no-deal? *Him.*" On the upside, however, he mused, it wouldn't be long before the bombastic Junkett sloganeering with which he was so familiar began to be deconstructed as the devils started to emerge from the detail of the Brussels tome and left traders on both sides of the Channel aghast at the amount of paperwork involved in selling anything to anyone until they gave up altogether.

"Stick *that* up what's left of your arse and try selling it to Mister and Missus Joe Public when the economy implodes," Norman muttered, clambering off his bunk and heading towards the driver's seat. It was one thirty a.m. and, having downed the better part of one of the last bottles of Plonque Française to be shipped through the port of Dover, Norman would have been better advised to stay in his bunk and go to sleep, but you know how it is when the booze renders you heroic and invulnerable. Quite apart from being less able to drive a motor vehicle than a baboon is to thread needles, Norman also had no memory of being in a Tier Four Covid zone from which no exit was allowed under any circumstances. Or of his chosen destination—Poole Dorset—being in a less restricted tier than London. But, as he had infamously done back in an earlier lockdown when breaking all the rules and driving up-country to Durham—"to get his eyes tested"—Norman reckoned rules were for the little people, not him.

Mind you, even no longer with a PM to hide behind, he might well have got away with his churlish arrogance on this occasion, too. It wasn't as if, unlike in Germany, Italy, France and elsewhere, the UK had ever managed to police its Covid restrictions to any meaningful effect, which was one of the reasons for the full-to-bursting hospitals and the appallingly high death rate. On the other hand, police do tend to take an interest in a Winnebago weaving across lanes along a motorway at speeds in excess of 120 kph while blaring its horn and causing a number of other vehicles to swerve about and barely avoid pile ups. By the time PCs Winston McCall and Billy Normington turned on the blue flashing lights and the wah-wahs and pedalled the metal, the local 999 emergency lines had been practically overwhelmed by anxious fellow motorists.

"Fuck," muttered Norman when he realised what was going on. But however hard you try, you can't make a Winnebago outrun a police BMW. Norman should have known that but what with one thing and another, didn't, and so just waved a two-finger salute through the driver's window while urging the Winnebago to speeds to which it had never aspired. That, understandably, was why it gave up the challenge, thereby causing its engine to hiss a lot before exploding and bringing its wheels to a skidding halt slap in the middle of the M27.

"Some dickhead," said Winston to Billy as their BMW drew up alongside.

"Let's just get him out of there nice and easy," said Billy. "Reckon we'll need the Taser?"

"Sure, just in case. Bloke's got to be out of his head," said Winston.

Even at *this* critical juncture, Norman Gubbins might have escaped the fate that awaited him. By claiming a mercy dash to a newly Covid-diagnosed elderly parent in a Poole care home, for example. But legless, still smarting over Junkett's Brexit crowing, and irritated by the Winnebago's breakdown, Norman wasn't at his fictional best, particularly not when also faced with gawping motorists crawling past while two surly coppers asked him to step down from his vehicle and produce his driver's licence. For one of *his* status, it was all very humiliating, which might have explained why he denied Winston and Billy their requests while simultaneously questioning their parentage. Well, as you can imagine, that didn't go down at all well with Winston and Billy, the latter eagerly fingering his Taser.

"We'll give you one last chance, sir," said Winston, who was a three-strikes-and-out type of policeman.

In retrospect, Norman really should have accepted this final opportunity for acquiescence and *not* tried to biff Winston on the nose, but you know how it is with the conditional perfect tense, how futile it is to look back in regret at all the could haves and should haves and might haves that make up our lives, because what's done is done and can't be undone.

*Any*way, that was the reason for Norman Gubbins being Tasered, slung into the back seat of the BMW and driven off to the local cop shop for the identification and further questioning that were to lead to the unearthing of not only his well-publicised illicit trip to Durham but sadly for him also the unfortunate violence at Sir Keith Staniford's secret Chelsea flat. Nor did his plea of having only recently been the

PM's most trusted advisor go down well with his interlocutors. In fact it went down little better than a bowl of cold sick or a lead parachute—pick your metaphor—given the odium in which 10 Downing Street and all in it were held. The dartboard in the local nick was superimposed with a back view mock-up of a naked Bruno Junkett grinning asininely over his shoulder. The winner of the game was the one who clustered all his or her darts in Junkett's bottom. Little could they have appreciated the ironies of the current situation as they remanded in custody the original artificer of prime ministerial half-arsedness pending further investigations, but they would have laughed if they'd known. Might even have let Norman off with a congratulatory slap on the back. Unless, of course, they had also known his motives, in which case the action would have been in line with everything else in his self-seeking existence.

Anyway, enough of these empty hypotheses. The facts of the matter were that Norman Gubbins was now up to his eyes in very deep doo-doo, which is where he would remain for the foreseeable future. Policepersons don't take kindly to being assaulted by anybody, let alone posturing pissed posh boys pretending pre-eminence.

~ *~

"Okay, so show 'em in," Dougal Klank told Hank O'Henry as Maggie McKenzie and Catya Rampersad put the final touches to their equipment in an anteroom. The girls had arrived back in Washington only two days earlier and were still reeling from The Siege of Capitol Hill, which had left them even keener on doling out to Klank their own brand of justice.

"With you in two," Hank called back.

"Two *WHUT*? Hours? Weeks? *YEARS*? I'm a busy guy," growled Klank, furious with Congress for finally announcing Bailey as president despite his best attempts to prevent it by promoting the worst insurrection of its kind in American history.

"Seconds, Mister President," Hank replied, settling the burger on its dish before spiking the Coke with six crushed Zipicione tablets and stirring well. "Just checking we have all in order here for the haircut of all haircuts for the man we believe to be the best president America ever had."

"You got *that* right, Hunk. That's how I won my landslide victory at the election."

"Of course, you did, Mister President. My gals're just putting the final touches to their outfits."

"Make 'em sexy," Klank grunted.

"You betcha," Hank called back, surveying Catya and Maggie who, grinning behind their BAILEY SUCKS masks, were both unclad apart from thongs and frilly pink diaphanous blouses. "Here we come."

Klank's tongue lolled and his eyes ogled as the girls sashayed towards him across the Square Office while Hank toted the goodies tray aloft behind them.

"Man, some haircut *this* is gonna be," said the worst leader the free world had ever had.

"Haircut *and* all that goes with it, Mister President," said Catya, winking over her shoulder as she slid her ass along the opposite side of the big desk.

"We were sooo sorry to hear about you being cheated out of your job," said Maggie, tweeking her left nipple. "You were the best president America ever…"

"*Am*," Klank retorted. "I *am* the best president."

Maggie giggled. "Slip of the tongue, but I'll make it up to you, promise."

"Sure you will, honey. So will your friend. I like threesomes."

Catya rolled her eyes with pleasure at the thought.

"You wanna leave me'n the gals alone here while we have our 'haircutting' session?" Klank told Hank, doing the inverted commas with his fingers.

Hank grinned and said, "Sure, only Mister President ordered a burger and a cola. Wouldn't want them going to waste, would we?"

"I guess not. Got to keep up my strength, right?" said Klank. "And that ain't all I gotta keep up," he added, stroking his crotch lubriciously.

"Indeed, Mister President. So, here come the *hors d'oeuvres*."

"Horse's doubries, eh, Hunk?"

"Indeed Mister President, and I would recommend you start with the cola. I added a little speciality of my own in recognition of the occasion."

"Not booze, Hunk. I don't do booze."

Hank tut-tutted appreciatively. "Of course not, Mister President. Just let us say a powder with little zing for extra pleasure," he said, while Catya and Maggie stroked *their* crotches with matching lubricity and winked a lot.

"Ookay, I'll try it," said Klank. "The 'haircut' should be fun, am I right?"

"You are right, Mister President. As always."

Klank nodded agreement with that before slugging back the cola in three big gulps and saying, "Okay, the burger can wait."

And indeed the burger *did* wait—forever as it happens—because once the Zipicione kicked in, Klank's head hit the desktop and the heavy snoring began, Maggie looked to Hank for the thumbs-up, which he straightaway returned and, while Catya watched on in glee, the haircut of all haircuts was underway. Which, with Maggie's clever fingers and the super-clippers set to number zero, took little more than ten minutes until Klank was as bald as the day he was (sadly) born.

"How soon before he wakes up?" Maggie asked Hank when the job was done.

"Enough time for you gals to get dressed and hightail it out of here."

"And you, Hank?" said Catya. "You are sticking around?"

"Until he comes to and looks in the mirror. I'll take photos for you guys and that uncle of yours down in New Orleans, then I'm out of here forever. Meanwhile, great job, girls. Now hit the road and stay safe, okay?"

In any other time but a pandemic, Catya and Maggie would have hugged and kissed Hank O'Henry for having facilitated Uncle Silas's original idea but, with Covid rampant because Klank had done nothing to stop it, all three merely elbow-bumped and blew air-kisses, By the time the ghastly screams began resounding around the White House terrifying its few remaining occupants, Catya and Maggie were out of earshot and long gone. It was left to Hank to investigate the cause of the noise, although he knew full where it was coming from.

"Some problem, Mister President?" he said, re-entering the Square Office.

"AAAAAAAAAGGGGGH," said a shiny-pated Dougal Klank who, on wibbly-wobbly legs and with a hideously distorted face, was swinging a golf club—a number nine iron Hank reckoned—in front of what once had been a wall mirror but was now a pile of shattered glass on the carpet.

"Guess you weren't too impressed with the haircut, huh, you fucking cocksucker," said Hank, who for years had been longing to call Klank a cocksucker to his face and was relishing the moment.

"FUUUUUUUUCCCCKKKKKK," Klank replied, thereby alarming the White House alarm system, which in its turn triggered urgent messages to the Pentagon such that within minutes the Square Office was stormed by men toting AK-47s demanding to know what the cause of the problem was.

"Looks to me like he's gone terminally crazy after losing the election," Hank told the leader of the group, who identified himself as Lieutenant Horatio (real name Max) Nelson.

"I guess so, after even the Capitol riots didn't get him what he wanted," opined Horatio/Max.

"Yeah, he's been moping around here feeling sorry for himself ever since. Then Twitter took his account away. Then there was the second of his impeachments with a trial upcoming. I figure it was all a bit heavy even for Mister Thick Skin. It could be how come he pulled out all his hair, or shaved it off or whatever."

"Bad loser, huh."

"The worst," Hank confirmed.

"The guy sure liked his hair, though. Strange he should've shaved it all off."

Hank shrugged. "Who can tell *what* a person will do when their mind goes AWOL?

"You got that right, Mister...?"

"O'Henry, Hank O'Henry. I'm his personal assistant around here," said Hank as Klank continued screaming foul oaths and took to hopping up and down on one leg while head-butting a wall. "Maybe you and your guys could calm him down a little?"

Nelson turned to his two underlings, Chuck O'Connor and Jeff Schmeichel, told them to put their weapons down and "pacify" the very-soon-to-be ex-president, which could have meant any number of things including knocking him cold with batons. But Chuck and Jeff went for tackling him around the knees to knock him over, then sitting on his chest.

"OOOOOOOOFFFFFF, AAAAGGGHHH,' Klank was saying until Jeff clamped a Covid-proof gloved hand over his mouth.

It probably would have been better for Klank if he *hadn't* bitten through the mitt and thereafter Jeff's finger, otherwise he wouldn't have got himself punched on the nose and been obliged to shriek "MUTHAFUCKA," but that's what he did.

Horatio/Max winced. "What you want us to do with him now, Hank?"

"Lock him up somewhere he can't do himself or anyone else any more harm. In a few days he's out of the White House anyway. You got padded cells over at the Pentagon?"

"Nope, but I know a place that has."

"So..." Hank was saying when, with a last ditch effort, Klank rolled over, dislodged Chuck and Jeff, did a lopsided runner for a conveniently open French window and threw himself out of it.

"Holy *shit*," said Horatio/Max, hurrying over and peering downwards.

For a second Hank O'Henry feared the spectacle of a dead Klank splayed face down on the concrete leaking blood. Dislike the guy though he may, such would not have been the desired outcome of the "haircut of all haircuts." But when he saw what *had* happened, he couldn't help but suppress a chuckle. What better punishment for the worst president America had ever had than that, on his way downwards to certain death, the belt on his trousers should snag on the branch of an American Chestnut and leave him dangling with both arms raised skywards and legs flailing. On his phone, Hank snapped the picture that would go viral and amuse social and regular media users for years to come. No cartoonist could have conceived of a more appropriate image.

"Be my witness and swear he wasn't pushed, he jumped, that's what you'll tell the press and Twitter and suchlike, right?" said Horatio/Max to Hank. The last thing the lieutenant needed was evidence of the kind of Army malpractice that could spur the fury of the Proud Boys and their ilk. Enough nationwide trouble was already expected on the day Jack Bailey was inaugurated.

"I'll swear to it on any Bible you hand me," said Hank. "It's the *truth*."

"Sure, but truth took one helluva beating in the Klank years. Fake news and all of that. Lotta folks still only believe what Klank told them to and he's a straight up-and-down liar."

"You got that right, Lieutenant," said Hank, peering down at Dougal Klank writhing and squirming in his tree while shrieking for the help that was not immediately forthcoming.

And Hank wasn't the only one peering. Out on Pennsylvania Avenue, a small but growing crowd of gawkers was already gathering, pointing, laughing, and taking photographs. Pretty soon they would be moved on by equally amused police officers, but the damage was already done. That Dougal Klank was batshit crazy was clearly to be seen, even by the likes of the Proud Boys and other far-right freaks. As advised in the prologue (see above) you can call it comeuppance, payback time, poetic justice, just deserts, anything you want.

~ * ~

Catya Rampersad, Maggie McKenzie, Hank O'Henry, Mattie Dupree, Silas Baudoin and his dog Rufus called it "victory" when they all met up down the Mississippi, but only among themselves. Of their part in the removal of Klank's hair, and thereby its owner, no word was ever spoken beyond the strict confines of Silas's cabin. Silas did write a song about it, though, and to his great joy when its lyrics were posted by Catya on social media they were included as background to a ten-minute cartoon movie of the White House self-defenestration incident on, would you believe it, JawJaw. Ramona was delighted, and wrote to Silas thanking him and asking for any other politically engaged songs he might have under his belt.

Which was how it came to be that, deep into what was supposed to be his dotage, Catya's Uncle Silas became the new hero of Black Lives Matter, BAME, PRIDE and other related movements, and even received recognition from Jack Bailey's new White House with a Congressional medal. Martin Luther King Jr. Silas Baudoin may not have been, but his words would linger long in the hearts of the dispossessed. Not that he paid the adulation too much mind. He was happy enough to stay where he was up his creek off the old Mississippi with his routine and his best friend, Rufus. What more could a man want in a world gone crazy? For the record, the new hero of civil rights was to live to the age of one hundred and six, still with the neck of the battered old Gibson in one hand and a pencil in the other.

Twenty-three

Mordecai the elf and Hazchem the metamorphic hound were as delighted as Silas Baudoin & Co. that their part in what they called the "Scalp Klank" plan had been such a success. After all, apart from the failure to change Gubbins' febrile mind and their assist in Catya and Maggie's love affair, this had been their only other recent incursion into human affairs. They were also pleased when they heard on EIH that Norman had been detained at Her Majesty's pleasure in a secure psychiatric unit on Dartmoor while tests were carried out on his mental stability and the potential danger they entailed of ever releasing him back into civilised society. In many ways, this fate mirrored that of Norman's erstwhile mentor, Sam Bundy, who was still locked away at his Coney Island facility awaiting the trial that could determine his residence for a significant part of the rest of his life. Maybe Klank would presidentially pardon him on his last day in office when he would doubtless want to pardon hundreds of other lawbreaker chums of his, but how much weight would such pardons carry from a person who was in the metaphorical sense out of his tree and, in the more literal one, stuck on a branch of it.

"So at least that's three of the bad boy populists taken care of," said Mordy, tamping FairyBac into their shared pipe.

"There're more in the world, Mord," Hazchem replied. "Like Ripyurpanzov, for example."

"True enough, my friend. But there's not a lot we can do about him. It was the West that was always our stomping ground, was it not?"

Hazchem, currently in Knight of the Realm mode, nodded.

"So we will have to leave old Igor to our agents in the East," Mordy concluded.

"Who may have learnt a lesson or two from what's been happening on our turf."

"One hopes so," said Mordy, adding a final perfectionist's tamp to the FairyBac. "But there is still the fourth of our bad boys to be taken into account."

"Junkett."

"Spot on. Who, from what we've recently seen, is creaming his jeans over the Brexit deal. Hyping it—and himself—to the skies to divert attention from his Covid foul-ups."

"About which, as we agreed, we can do nothing," said Hazchem, as Mordy passed him the pipe for ignition. That was Hazchem's job with the pipe. He just did it better than Mordy.

"Quite. But one has to admit the self-congratulation is beyond irksome," said Mordy, flicking on the Elf Information Highway monitor which was showing repeat images of a smirking Bruno Junkett pen in hand at his desk in 10 Downing Street ready to sign away forever the UK's membership of the European Union it had been a part of for nigh on fifty years, the union originally formed in 1957 as the the European Economic Community, partly to ensure there would never again be a European war like the one ended just over a decade earlier.

"Yuck," said Hazchem. "It's enough to make you throw up your dinner. No more free movement around Europe, especially for Erasmus students, no more reciprocal medical care, no more..."

"No more many good things for the English, Hazza old chap. But plenty of bad ones—restrictions, mountainous incomprehensible paperwork for business, airport queues, et-cet-er-a, et-cet-er-*a*."

"You say 'the English,'" said Hazchem, finishing off the pipe lighting with his usual aplomb.

Mordy nodded and raised a hirsute old eyebrow. "Indeed I do. If you were a Scottish, Irish, or Welsh person, would *you* be happy to share in such deprivation and hassle, especially when signed off by a self-serving narcissist with certified bottom and brain problems and a peculiar non-haircut?"

Hazchem shook his head as he handed over the pipe. "No way, José."

"Quite. If *I* were any of those folk, I'd been looking for independence."

"The break-up of the UK?"

"Precisely. Northern Ireland could easily enough join up with the South, make one solid state and stay in the EU. The Scottish National Party have been demanding their freedom for years, and as for the Welsh, they have their own culture and might be happy enough to wave two fingers at the English in order to preserve it. What kind of a position would *that* leave Junkett in when he jabbers about world-class business deals all across the planet?"

"Fucked," said Hazchem, who reserved such words only for special occasions.

"Fucked indeed. And because not only would he be left with merely a tiny unproductive fiefdom to boss around, but also, as a Little Englander buffoon, would not have the charisma or statesmanship to do deals with any other country on earth. You will have seen some of the responses from overseas commentators already."

"No," said Hazchem.

"Well, how about this from *Der Spiegel* only a few days ago? The UK has been 'captured by frivolous clowns and liars,' it said. "And went on to brand Junkett 'a shameful rogue.' You can hear similar views from many quarters and not just in Europe. For example, this from an ex-UK Foreign Office minister quoted in *The Guardian* as having described Junkett as an 'embarrassing buffoon' with an untidy mind and sub-zero diplomatic judgement. Somebody who needs 'a regular fix of headlines and equates it with political power.'"

"He was elected PM, though," said Hazchem, watching on with pleasure as Mordy puffed luxuriantly on the newly lit pipe, then passed it back.

"Yes, but why? Because he was a good vote winner for the tired old Tories on the Brexit ticket, that was why. And sure enough, he delivered *those* goods and got the party elected with a big majority. But that was *all* he was capable of, *vide* the catastrophic handling of the Covid crisis. The man couldn't organise a piss-up in a brewery or two marbles to roll down a hill, never mind how much he bangs on about inoculating the entire UK population with anti-Covid vaccines, which still beg questions long-term, however initially effective they may be. That has been his escape route from both responsibility for over a hundred thousand Covid deaths and Brexit criticism, right? And *this* is the creature about to lead England into a brave new 'green' world of boundless wealth and commerce? I don't think so, Hazza. I... do...not...think...so. He's all blether and blabber and no substance and would be laughed off the world's stage. Klank he could have no doubt done deals with, but with President Bailey, a man of conscience?" said Mordy, passing the pipe back to Hazchem.

"I see where you're going," said Hazchem, toking hard.

"And none of the receding hair-lined brain-dead sycophants in his cabinet are sufficiently *pro*active to choose different neckwear each day, let alone organize a coherent long-term plan for anything, *vide* the shambles over the entire Covid story. These are *re*active fools without plans, fools who watch on as events unfold, then claim they've learnt lessons and are doing something about them when it's far too late. Fools without foresight, in other words. Led by a clown with the emotional age of six who strives day in and day out to be the most popular boy in the playground by being funny and is ooh-sooo-sorry when he has to pass on bad news. Pass the pipe, would you? I'm getting a little frazzled here."

"And *still* there's nothing we can do."

"Hazza, were it in our power, I would find a way to promote Sir Keith Staniford immediately into Downing Street. There he is, a wise, modest and eloquent lawyer, waiting in the wings, possibly *too* wise, modest and eloquent, you might say. But so to do, we would have to meddle with the entire British electoral system, which is doable for sure but, as I said, beyond our remit."

"So, we just sit around here and wait for the situation to unravel while half-arsed Junkett plays out his Mister Vaccine game as a diversion from even more serious matters? As if Brexit weren't serious enough."

"Actually no, Hazza, we don't just wait and wonder."

"What then?"

"We look to the future and see what *it* holds, something we elves find difficult as we tend to be locked in the present. But you may remember our helpmate in these circumstances."

"Afraid not," said Hazchem, whose memory was pretty much a thing of the past.

Which was when Mordy reminded him of Phoebe the Future Fairy, the only one of her kind ever blessed with any inkling of what tomorrow might hold. Not in any detail, of course, that would be asking far too much. Nonetheless she was always useful when it came to predictions of what just *might* be happening. Many moons ago, she and Mordy had enjoyed a brief but intense liaison to which neither ever referred, given that for elves the past was as much of another planet as the future.

"Get her up on screen, if you would be so good."

"Okay dokey," said Hazchem, fiddling with their EIH equipment. "She got an app?"

"A *what*?" said Mordy, a technophobe to his ageless bones.

"Never mind, just let me scroll around."

"Scroll away, old friend, and let me know when you've found her."

While Hazchem fiddled and scrolled, Mordy allowed his old head to loll. Across all the years, he had witnessed many dreadful human situations, but nothing compared with those of the year 2020. Okay, it had taken a malign bug to bring the world to its knees and millions to their deaths but what, he wondered, were the factors that underpinned the current disaster. Without having to think all that much, he reduced them to two:

1) The blithe yet arrogant insouciance that gave humans to believe they ruled the planet, were immune to such events as pandemics, and therefore saw no reason to obey the rules proposed to counter the

danger they were in. The richer they were, the less they obeyed *any* rules and thereby got even richer while the poor with no access to defences got even poorer or died. In economics, this was called the K factor.

And,

2) The rapacious greed over centuries with which homo "sapiens" had ravaged, despoiled and devastated Nature to the point at which it could no longer function or sustain the needs of homo capitalist and indeed might kill him off altogether through global warming. There was also speculation that coronavirus itself may have resulted from previously unheard-of bugs being freed from their normal habitat through deforestation.

"Maybe, just maybe," Mordy mused, "Covid is Nature's revenge. And I wish Her well with the project."

It was Hazchem saying, "I got her, Mord, I got her. Here comes Phoebe," that shook Mordecai from his ruminations and caused him to look up and see his old lover on the EIH screen in the fairy version of what humans called Zoom.

"Phoebe, hi there," he said.

"Mordy, what a pleasure, how *are* you these days, my dear?" said Phoebe with a wink of the kind that caused Hazchem to raise an eyebrow. Hazchem knew nothing of Mordecai's love life, always having assumed he'd never had one, but that wink told its own tale. Not that he could blame his oldest, best, and only friend. Whatever her age, Phoebe was a stunner in anybody's book.

"Oh, you know, battling on as usual," said Mordy, blushing slightly at Hazchem's eyebrow raising and determining it best to get down to business rather than dwelling on times past. Had there been progeny from the relationship, he would have known about it by now but there had been no word of such events from Phoebe, so...

"And how may I be of assistance?" said the Future Fairy goddess, intuiting Mordy's mini-dilemma and sparing him any further embarrassment.

Which was when a grateful Mordy cut to the chase with a brief résumé of his and Hazchem's recent concerns in the Western Zone, with which Phoebe was already *au fait*, before posing the key question about Junkett.

"For how much longer," he asked Phoebe, "will this mindless, pro-Klank, bullshitting moron remain in ten Downing Street?"

"Aha," said Phoebe. "A little bird told me, and don't ask me how she knew, you would soon be in touch hoping for an answer to that question. This is the certified brain-dead, half-arsed, populist, narcissistic prime minister of Great Britain we're talking about here, right?"

"Indeed so, my dear," said Mordy, causing Hazchem to smile.

"Sooo, let me look into my future annals. But do remember, Mordy, I am unable to pinpoint with any accuracy the exact *dates* of any of the events that may occur down the line or details as to their cause. All I can offer is a wide-screen picture suggesting glimpses and outlines of situations at *some* time in the future without any specific indication as to their causes. Will you be happy with that?" said Phoebe, rubbing at her computerised crystal ball.

"As Larry," said Mordy. "More I would have never expected. Perhaps I should give you a reminder of what our target looks like."

"Indeed, that would be helpful."

"Medium height, pudgy, late fifties, flat face with slanting eyebrows and lying eyes, bog-brush dyed yellow hair with bald patches, perpetual delusional smirk on his lips. Does that help?"

"Indeed, it does. O*okay* then, here we go," said Phoebe, before muttering the magic words, "Crystie, Crystie here's a mystery," then whispering Bruno's name and description and asking what might be surmised about his current position in life.

While this was happening, Mordy and Hazchem passed the pipe back and forth and pretended to be thinking about something else, a pretence they had to maintain for a nerve-wracking twenty-six minutes until Phoebe came back on line.

"Any luck?" asked Mordy.

Phoebe grinned. "For whom?"

"You, in your quest."

"Yes, there is information. But first may I confirm for perspective's sake what your stance in regard to this Junkett person is? Friend or foe?"

"The latter, very obviously," Mordy readily admitted.

"Okay, thanks. Then your luck's in and his is out."

"Raaf, raaf, *raaf*," said Hazchem, reverting to canine terms in his excitement.

"As I said, there are no hard and firm facts regarding his current position, but I can report that as of sometime in the not too distant future he is no longer seen to be inhabiting number ten Downing Street. It's misty, but there are indications from the look of his private office he is no longer the regular occupant of it."

Mordy and Hazchem leapt from their seats and hi-fived, which was quite safe seeing as they were immune from coronavirus.

"Any idea who might have replaced him?" said Mordy, when the hi-fiving was over.

"Just hold on a mo," said Phoebe, whispering at Crystie again.

She was back on line a nail-biting ten minutes later. "I have no names. All I can tell you it is likely to be a man, not a woman. From the team photo on the wall, I would assume he takes an interest in the game humans call soccer."

Mordy and Hazchem looked at each other and raised hopeful eyebrows. "And of Junkett himself you have no identifying picture?"

"Only one that Crystie claims to be the most recently available image, but of which I'm still uncertain. Would you care to see it?"

"Indeed we would," said Hazchem.

"Okay. Give me a second while I ask Crystie to get it back up."

The second lapsed into three hundred and twenty-five seconds by the time Phoebe had retrieved it from Crystie, but the wait was well worthwhile, for once the image hit the screen Mordy and Hazchem whooped, clapped, and chortled.

"That him?" said Phoebe. "So much excitement."

"To a T, my dear," said Mordy, as he and Hazchem watched the video images of a tearful Bruno Junkett pedalling his bike no hands around what looked a lot like St James's Park until, letting go of the handlebars to clutch his left buttock with one hand and his hair with the other while swerving back and forth, his front wheel fell off and he tumbled head first into the lake.

"It's the best Crystie can do, will it suffice?" said Phoebe.

"Indeed it will, my dearest, and thank you *so* much," said Mordy, when the whooping, clapping, and chortling were over. "For reasons you don't need to know, it appears to suggest a fitting end to a particularly nasty chapter in British history."

Once Phoebe was back off air after blowing kisses at her erstwhile paramour, Mordy and Hazchem lay back on their easy chairs and enjoyed a fresh pipe of FairyBac.

"Well, that seems to be the fourth of the bad boy populists off the scene," said Hazchem.

Mordy chuckled. "One certainly hopes as much. I particularly enjoyed the wheel falling off before the header into the briny. Portentous metaphors indeed."

"A suicide attempt?" said Hazchem.

"I think not. Narcissists don't kill themselves, especially not by purposefully loosening their bicycle's front wheel and doing a header into a relatively shallow lake. Remember Klank with his short-lived Hemingway moment. But at least we can assume mental fragmentation occasioned by rejection of some sort, which is in and of itself a hopeful sign.

"Baaaaaaa!" agreed Samantha, who'd joined the party late but enjoyed what she'd seen. What "meeatyfors" were, let alone portentous ones, she had no idea, but who cared as long as in Junkett's case they signalled something bad. She'd never been a fan of either him or the cretins who'd thought he was funny and voted for him. Like humans' idea of sheep they'd behaved. Mercifully, *real* sheep were a whole lot more intelligent.

Post Scriptum

March/April 2021

As stated in the Prologue, the factional/fictional events of this piece refer solely to the *annus horribilis* 2020 closing, as is the way with years, on the 31st of December. Obviously enough, however, history did not stop there, hence the need for a brief update on the fates of the central players in the early New Year. Obviously enough, Dougal Klank did not remain forever hanging in a tree by his trouser belt, nor did Bruno Junkett drown in St. James's Park lake after falling off his bike. In case you hadn't guessed it already, such wish-list fates were merely examples of the fictional aspect of this account. So what *did* happen to them in the early days of 2021?

Well, as you will doubtless know by now, both survived the opprobrium doled out to them—Dougal Klank lost the presidential election, but was nonetheless acquitted at his second impeachment trial, meaning he was free to stand again in 2024 and Junkett was *not* kicked out of Downing Street for terminal fecklessness, so both remain in positions of national relevance, despite their previous failures to either recognize or manage the rampages of coronavirus.

Klank and members of his sect including close family are busy selling MAGA products and appearing before sell-out crowds around the USA in the very real hope of reversing the result of the 2020 election next time around, thereby already constituting a major thorn—more like dagger—in Jack Bailey's side/heart. In the pursuit of such glory, Klank has even overcome the initial despair of baldness by disclosing it publicly to nobody and sporting daily, as Uncle Silas had predicted, the fanciest of perukes in town.

In the UK, Junkett, unsurprisingly, is currently taking personal credit for the hugely successful vaccination campaign for the organisation and administration of which the National Health Service deserves the accolades. But they're not getting them, because Bruno has hijacked NHS glory and is currently riding the crest of the populist wave engendered by the campaign, swaggering about the land elbow bumping people as if *he* were not only the inventor of the Oxford AstraZenica jab but also its most prolific jabber. This despite repeated allegations of sleaze, financial wrongdoings, and having been overheard late in 2020 outside the Cabinet Room saying he'd prefer "bodies to pile high in their thousands" rather than have "yet another fucking lockdown." Plus there is now the question of who paid for renovations to the 10 Downing Street apartment or "Flatgate" as the wittier media have dubbed it. Such character slurs might eventually see the end of our Bruno. But such is the fickleness of public memory— what Paul Simon refers to in "Call Me Al" as "a short little span of attention"—that Junkett may still survive. Especially as he has finally kicked the Gubbins habit and got himself some new advisers, who have infinitely more sensible ideas about handling pandemics. Not that they are given any credit for their acumen, of course, they might just as well not exist as far as public opinion is concerned, all plaudits for the falling death toll being garnered and treasured by Teflon Bruno, who has drawn a very firm line under the fuck-ups of 2020 and is now basking in the sorts of glory best suited to his narcissism and hoping to remain PM for the foreseeable. Anyway, buoyed by such success, Junkett has even learnt to manage his (fictional) left buttock problem with a special strap so he no longer falls over unexpectedly.

In the light of such developments, the person standing most to lose is Sir Keith Staniford, however much he tries to make of Flatgate. The percipient questions that had once so frightened Bruno at Prime Minister's Question Time no longer do so, because Junkett simply alludes to the vaccination roll out, pats himself on the back, and ignores Staniford altogether. This inability any longer to snipe at Junkett and repeatedly demand clarity rather than waffle has left the Labour leader with something of a problem—namely to invent on the hoof Labour party policies even remotely capable of competing with Junkett's runaway Covid jab jollies, which are already beginning to eat into and reverse Sir Keith's erstwhile narrow lead in the popularity polls. It is almost as though the average voter *prefers* a vainglorious criminal buffoon running the country to a worthy but boring ex-lawyer.

As for Sam Bundy, who *was* pardoned by Klank on his last day in power, and Norman Gubbins, who was eventually released from his (fictional) custody, there is no further information, although it can safely be assumed they are skulking around somewhere in the shadows profiting from whatever mayhem they can still create. In the factual Gubbins' case, by sowing the seeds of Flatgate.

On a happier note, Jack Bailey is busy successfully fighting Covid-19 across the USA, restoring positive relationships with all those organisations and nations Klank had scorned, spurned or spited, and pouring trillions of dollars into domestic health and redevelopment schemes designed to benefit the poorest in society. He is particularly grateful in these projects not only for the help and support of his new team, but especially, on a day-to-day basis in the White House, for the care taken of him by (the fictional) Hank O'Henry and Catya Rampersad, who are relishing their new responsibilities.

Where love ties are concerned, Catya and Maggie are contemplating wedlock, as are George and Belinda (later to become the parents of a large brood, see above), while the power relations in the marriage of Ramona and Rickie/Enrique/Henry have been reversed, such that following the success of her half-arsed Junkett posts, Ramona is now the boss of JawJaw while Rickie/Enrique/Henry is considering a new career as late night spook radio host.

Which leaves Silas Baudoin, who throughout this narrative has never left his Mississippi creek despite his new international reputation as the voice of Black Lives Matter and BAME. And then, of course, there are Mordecai and Hazchem back in their Lakeland home caring for their sheep while keeping a weather eye open for any future interventions in their power to avert terminal human fecklessness. A shame Silas, Rufus, Mordy, and Hazchem were never able to meet up in person, because they would surely have got along like a house on fire. Maybe some sunny day, like families riven by coronavirus, they will. Mordy plays a pretty mean tin whistle, and Hazchem the bongos, so they could make a band. After all, The Beatles had to start somewhere. A person is free to dream.

Meet Paddy Bostock

Paddy Bostock was born in Liverpool and holds a B.A. in Modern Languages and History, a PGDip TESL, and a PhD in English Literature. Down the years, he has been a barman, a road worker, a songwriter, an educational researcher, a translator, a book reviewer, a university lecturer and Chair of Department, and a high school mentor. He lives in London and likes animals and bicycles.

Other Works From The Pen Of
Paddy Bostock

Mole Smith and the Diamond Studded Pistol – Only one way for PI gofer Mole Smith to win the hand of his beloved: to solve the ancient mystery of the diamond-studded pistol…

Two Down – Worry about your cellphone! Others may have spooky designs on it…

La Joie de Vivre – "Cherchez la femme!"—words Ambler will come to wish he'd never heard…

For the Love of a Woman – Family—you can't live with them; you can't live without them.

Foot Soldiers – When will we ever learn…?

Hand in Glove – Never judge a zebra by its stripes…

Noddy in Wonderland – Will wonders never cease?

Peace on Earth – Peace on earth? Don't bet on it.…

The Basque Head Case – Of heads found…and lost!…

The Bore – Funny thing, boredom…

The Hanging – Nothing is set in stone.

Chosen – It's only rock 'n' roll but…

What Ifs – "We are such stuff as dreams are made on…"

Fubars – Serendipity works in mysterious ways…

My Kind of Guy – Even when you can't move mountains, you might still create a few shock ripples…

The Showdown in Wollongong – Love should come with a health warning.

Letter to Our Readers

Enjoy this book?

You can make a difference

As an independent publisher, Wings ePress, Inc. does not have the financial clout of the large New York Publishers. We can't afford large magazine spreads or subway posters to tell people about our quality books.

But, we do have something much more effective and powerful than ads. We have a large base of loyal readers.

Honest Reviews help bring the attention of new readers to our books.

If you enjoyed this book, we would appreciate it if you would spend a few minutes posting a review on the site where you purchased this book or on the Wings ePress, Inc. webpages at

https://wingsepress.com/

Thank You